MW00570320

LET GO
THE GLASS
VOICE

Let Go the GLASS Voice

by
Maureen McCafferty

Livingston Press
The University of West Alabama

ISBN 0-942979-27-3, Cloth (library binding)
ISBN 0-942979-28-1, Paperback

Library of Congress CIP # 97-71805
Manufactured in the United States of America.
First Edition
Copyright © 1997 by Maureen McCafferty

Acknowledgements: parts of this novel have appeared in slightly altered
forms in the following magazines:
Rhino (as "grave things")
Arizona Mandala (as "Holy Bird Cures")
The author wishes to thank Dr. Joe Taylor and the staff of Livingston Press.

Typesetting and layout: Joe Taylor
Proofreading: Beth Grant, Geoff Hodge, Lee Holland-Moore, Cindy Slimp,
and Tricia Taylor
Artwork: Cover by Brandon Kershner
First four Celtic motifs from *Celtic Motifs* by Mallory Pearce,
copyrighted by Dover Publications. Used in accordance to Dover's
copyright notice.
Final Celtic motif is an adaptation from *The Book of Kells*.

Livingston Press
"Specializing in off-beat and Southern literature"
Other works of interest are listed in the back of this book.
For a complete listing, write
Livingston Press
Station 22
The University of West Alabama
Livingston, AL 35470

LET GO
THE GLASS
VOICE

*For my family, in memory of my grand-
fathers, Patrick McMahon and Phillip
McCafferty, whose stories are still being told and ever improved upon by my
grandmothers: Elizabeth McMahon and
Cassie McCafferty*

I. *The Daoine Sidhe and Some Ancient Family Cures*

When Nora Cavanaugh was about five, her mother and grandfather started telling Nora about God. They had different reasons. And they had different gods. Nora's grandfather had friendly gods: the ancient Celtic spirits—the *daoine sidhe,* the shadowgods of the earth who loved song and dance like Granhugh, Nora's grandfather. The shadows had and wanted no powers but the ones Granhugh, Hugh Logan, had and wanted too: transformation and healing. In Granhugh's stories, the shadows healed sorrow by transforming people, usually into birds. "And then the world was theirs," Granhugh always said, envying such boundlessness, maybe the only thing he ever did envy; at ninety-one he still hated boundaries, of all kinds.

Nora listened to the shadow stories carefully enough to know that the birdpeople were the lucky ones. There were also stories of pigpeople who didn't fly or escape. Nora's grandfather heard these stories from his own father, Mick Logan, who heard them from his father and mother when he was a boy in County Monaghan, in Ireland. Like his fathers and mothers before him, Hugh Logan is a *seanachai*, a storyteller, a transformer of the world around him. "We knew the shadow world because we lived near a ringfort, the shadows' burial ground, holy ground, you see," Hugh Logan told his granddaughter. He wanted Nora to know the world he came from, which was the world she came from too, even if she'd never seen it. He told Nora that even the things she could see wouldn't be the whole story or always easy to understand.

He told her, for instance, that when he was about her age he saw a transformation— "a wondrous though dangerous thing to be witnessing, for you could be enchanted away yourself without much trouble. A song or a look and then you'd be gone forever," he told her, very seriously, because these were very serious things he was revealing. "Living with the fairies, you'd be, which might not be so bad but people never wanted to see it happen, don't you know."

But it did.

"The ringfort was between our farm and the next which belonged to the Kellys. No one farmed the land, of course, or trespassed either, but we sometimes saw the shadows there and the shadows saw us. The shadows had been watching the Logans and Kellys for generations. So they knew that the Kellys were always having troubles, the way some families do. One of the Kellys was *always* dying tragically or being born wrong or dead. There was just no luck," Granhugh said. "But the Kellys went on and on with life as strange as it was for them, except the youngest boy Liam.

"He was dreamy and melancholy, and the shadows, you see, don't mind mischief but they can't abide sadness, especially in children." About here Granhugh usually filled his pipe, letting Nora pack down the tobacco with her thumb as he told her, "One night when it was very dark and everyone was asleep, didn't I go out into damp air, which was no small risk—my mother could be fierce if you crossed her. *Hanam an diabhail, Your soul to the devil*, she'd say to scare us children till we figured out she wouldn't be sending us to any devil unless she was ready to go herself. But still I knew not to go out into the foggy night and I wouldn't have been there at all if I hadn't had the feeling that I was supposed to witness something, which might have been part of the *daoine sidhe* spell, don't you know.

"And wasn't I out there seeing nothing at all till I spotted this flash of light and then this stream of light through the trees that I couldn't do anything but walk to, the spell was that strong. The mysterious color with the blue edges was pulling me to it, right into the ringfort. That's where I was I tell you, about to step into that holy place, to be enchanted away when I stopped. And what do you think I saw but young Liam Kelly in the middle of the strange light, standing right there as if nothing was happening. It was dangerous I tell you. If the *sidhe* had wanted me then, I'd have been gone without moving a step from where I was. Nothing to be done about it but to keep watching Liam and you know what I saw, Norie?" Granhugh asked every time as Nora held her breath, picturing the young boy who was her grandfather out in the foggy night about to be lost into the shadow spell. "You know what I saw?" he asked, waiting for no answer. "I saw the most remarkable thing—that Liam wasn't afraid. Surrounded by all those dancing shadows, he wasn't afraid or sad or even worried. He was happy. Dancing with the music, he was so free and happy it already wasn't Liam I was watching. Then it *really* wasn't Liam. In a flash, an instant that almost bolted me over, I saw Liam's scrawny little boy body suddenly sleek into a beautiful strong full black *bird*. One instant. Fantastic thing. Don't think such things can't happen. They happen whether you see them or not, Noriegirl," Hugh Logan told his granddaughter. "The shadows saved Liam that night. They blew a breath and Liam soared." Nora liked to picture that.

She liked most of her grandfather's stories which meant to warn her: *Never trust only what you see. It's never the whole story*. And also, the *daoine sidhe* will watch out for you if you let them. He told Nora to let them.

Her mother's stories were wild and wonderful too, and though her mother's God didn't sing or dance, there were stories of miracles and floods and arks and in church there were stained glass pictures of these things as well as the smell of hundreds of burning candles, and some days incense. All this for one God. Nora's mother, Mary Cavanaugh, who grew up in the Bronx, some parts of Manhattan, Brooklyn and then Queens where the Cavanaughs and Logans still lived, said there was only one God. And you wouldn't see Him living in the backyard, no matter how early you got up. The mystery was that the one God was two men and a holy bird spirit. No women. The two men and the holy bird were all rolled into each other but separate: the Holy Trinity. The mystery for Nora was that there was a Father and Son but no Mother-God. She asked her mother how there could be no mother but the baby Jesus could be God, and Nora's mother told her about *faith*, saying the word as if it were holy and secret. Nora didn't understand it all but she liked the stories of The Holy Mother even if she wasn't a God, and Nora secretly thought that there had been some mistake about this. Mary Cavanaugh also told her daughter that the Holy Mother was good to pray to because she could take a message to God or her Son, Jesus. They didn't appear much but apparently accepted messages. But there weren't any stories about the two-man God or even the holy bird spirit transforming anyone Nora's mother knew. Mary Cavanaugh's God was more serious than that, and Mary Cavanaugh was too, though she hadn't always been.

In Nora's earliest memories, her mother wasn't serious about anything but her painting, her picnics (which she sometimes took Nora out of school to have), and her friend, Lillian Bead. Nora's mother had known Lillian Bead since they were kids in the Bronx. Lillian lived a long subway-ride away but Nora remembered Lillian often coming to visit them. She made Nora's mother happy. They went on picnics and to parks and just did things with each other, or even if they didn't, even if Lillian spent the day having coffee with Nora's mother and talking—Lillian had a husband and two sons she told very funny stories about—she had a way of talking that cheered Mary Cavanaugh. Lillian could make you picture her words when she talked, like Granhugh. She had a different sound from Granhugh, but she had the same confidence; she didn't question her own ways. Mary Cavanaugh doubted almost everything about herself and her world. Nora suspected that Lillian had saved her mother a few times from her awful sadness. When Nora's sister Hallie was born, Lillian was godmother, though they hadn't seen much of Lillian by then.

That was the beginning of the bad times for Nora's mother. She'd given up her friend Lillian and talked to God a lot, who, in Mary Cavanaugh's world, sounded an awful lot like Nora's very serious grandmother, Nonny.

If Nora hoped anything to be true about whatever gods there really were, wherever they were, it was that they had more mercy than her grandmother.

Nora never chose a god. She didn't have to. Her mother assumed Nora believed her, while her grandfather assumed his version of things was favored, and her grandmother didn't really care what god you believed in as long as you appeared to believe her version of family events. She assumed Nora did. All their assumptions were founded. Nora believed in all and yet in none of these worlds. That's how it was growing up in Nora's family, all stories real and unreal at the same time. God and gods, shadows and charms, sins, secrets, and ancient cures pervaded the stories and voices. All real in a world where you never knew what was real, or not. And mostly you didn't try to find out.

*

Nora is nearly thirty years old, hasn't lived at home for almost two years, and the odd thing, she thinks, is that the longer she's away, the more tangled she is in the spiderweb of stories that have shaped most of her life. She sees the events of her life as stories because that's what they have been turned into, mostly by Nora's grandmother, which is a story in itself. All Nora knows is that wander too far into these stories or events and there's no way out: you're stuck in the sticky, seductive lines, the poisonous half-truths, untruths, the curling, corrupted design, the place where the past is everywhere, yet concealed.

And the present? About all Nora knows about the present is that she's been walking all night (driven into it, like her grandfather, by a keen feeling), with nothing to follow but the road in front of her and maybe the pull of the moon that lets Nora see there's nothing to see anywhere but snow, woods and the line of road that runs through them.

She puts her gloved hands under her arms and her head down against the wind. All she really remembers is that her mother called last night and said something about the dead which was strange since it is usually Nora's grandfather who warns about the dead. Maybe her mother was telling her about a dream. Her mother has very powerful, prophetic dreams. One of the most disturbing is the baby fish dream: "There was this fish; it was big and powerful and angry and people thought it was dangerous, but I knew it was a baby," her mother told Nora not long ago. "For a while in the dream people chased the baby fish, trying to harpoon or even shoot it, and finally from exhaustion it washed up on the beach. I thought it would rest and be okay but it was in trouble and people didn't know what to do; they wanted to kill it because it was suffering and they couldn't stand it. Don't let people see how you suffer, Nora," her mother advised. "They won't be able to stand it, or you." A few days later she called again. "Your cousin Eugene's in trouble," Mary Cavanaugh had figured out from the dream. "Real trouble."

Nora's cousin Eugene will be nineteen in only four days. It's an accomplishment—Eugene's had to make his way through nineteen years of trouble, but he's more settled now. The last time her mother talked to Eugene something seemed settled between them. When was that? It seems like such a long time since Nora's seen him; it makes her sad.

Strange sounds echo in the eerie light that reveals only patches of the empty road Nora takes through the woods. It would be easy to die here, she thinks, surprised by the thought, not wanting all these thoughts about death (not wanting to think about the soreness she knows is a nasty bruise just under her left breast). "It's the light," she tells herself. "Everything looks strange." She wishes her grandfather were here.

Suddenly Nora is reassured by remembering her friend Renie. That's where I'm headed, to Renie's house. She wonders how she could forget such a thing, picturing her memory as a glass bubble that has been thrown in the air and exploded, pieces of it falling everywhere. I'll have to collect the shards when they land, she thinks, picturing her hands going through the snow for the hidden slivers of glass, cutting herself on them. How did this happen? One minute everything was fine. I was in my apartment, settled on the sofa in my bathrobe, reading, on a quiet night, when the phone rings, and in a second, without warning, everything has changed; in a second I'm pulling on jeans, sweater, coat, boots and running.

She tries to touch her left side as if this will heal or comfort the injured skin somehow, but she only feels the soreness of twisting to reach what she can't feel in her heavy coat. Nora wants to think it's the wind and night that's disorienting her usually clear and controlled mind. She wants to think that her mind is usually clear and almost always in control of what she does. "Don't fool with the dead," she tells herself. Her grandfather's advice. She's speaking out loud because talking seems to keep the other sounds inside her from erupting and disrupting her progress. She likes to think she's making progress. She thinks there's such a thing.

That's probably her grandmother's voice. All Nora knows of her grandmother is that she left Ireland with nothing when she was seventeen to come to America where she knew no one. *I had a hard time, everyone does. Don't be crying about your troubles.* That is surely her grandmother's voice. It's very deep in Nora. It's the voice that suggests, though never directly, that adversity is not a bad thing as long as you fight it and maintain your dignity which mostly consists of silence. The good thing about struggle, this voice always says, is that it's hard to remember even things you're afraid of if you're using all your energy to keep from being swept into a storm, any storm. It's a little trick Nora has learned from her grandmother: make things physically hard on yourself (go out on a cold windy night with yourself so bruised you can barely walk), and you'll forget pains of the heart or mind. It works most of the time. But Nora's beginning to see drawbacks: pain, for one, exhaustion for another. And yet it's true: it's hard to remember things you're afraid of if you're using all your energy to keep from being swept into the story. *The story?* Yes, everything in her family is made into a story. I'm in the middle of one now, Nora thinks. I'm in one of Nonny's stories.

Nora can tell by the force of the thing (the thing her mother has told her last night which she can't remember) that this is one her grandmother's stories. Almost everything in their family is known by her grandmother's story of it. It was Nonny's story that Nora's cousins Sheila and Kathleen were twins, that Granhugh was their grandfather, that Aunt Peg's husband Arthur was her second husband, that Nora's mother, Mary, went to Paris for a year when Nora was about eleven. There was even a story about

Nora's father (who was usually left alone and out of the picture), but Nonny had stories about Ed Cavanaugh too when she needed them. The one Nora remembers is that years ago Nora's father had taken some money from Nonny (which he never did) and gambled it on a horse (which he also never did), losing the down payment on a house meant for Aunt Peg. All of these stories, and so many more, were tangled threads in a crazycrazy design that had very little truth in it. (Except what it told you about Nonny, part of which was that truth was never really an important ingredient, for her purposes, and that her purposes were everywhere.)

For a while, Nora's mother supplied competing versions of events and experiences, but the competition became brutal and Nora's mother withdrew.

Someone laughs. Not Nora.

More voices? Her head is full of them. She's heard voices for years. The way anyone does who has a clue that there is a world inside the world you see where voices and memories wander. Nora supposes these voices have a purpose, other than to erupt now and then. Inside her head.

It has to do with the light, she tells herself again. When Nora and her sister Tessa were small, there were nights, usually when their father was working late and something about the twilight disturbed their mother, when Mary Cavanaugh would tolerate no light but a few candles. Sometimes she would light the candles and keep Nora and Tessa near to soothe herself. And as their mother felt comforted, it calmed the girls too. Sometimes, more than anything else in the world seen or unseen, Nora wants to crawl back to that time, to that quiet house with the soft light and curl beside her mother.

She is numb with cold, and yet too warm to go on. Her clothes feel heavy. She wants to take off her big black coat and her heavy sweater but she doesn't; she keeps walking, knowing now that someone is following her, even suspecting who (though he's dead).

She will not think about this. She wants to be somewhere else, someone else. For a second, she considers becoming someone else, slipping into a new name, personality, reality. Why not? Her grandmother's had many names, and at least several personalities. For a second, this seems possible. I don't even have to get on a big ship and sail three thousand miles, Nora thinks, feeling she can just begin now, from nothing, from everything that is suddenly new in her somehow with this voice that is telling her that she doesn't have to be Nora Cavanaugh anymore. But in the same second that she hears and feels this pull, this temptation to be safe and new and pure and holy and all the other things she wants to be right now, in that same instant, Nora also feels some affection, some saving affection for Nora Cavanaugh, as if she is not Nora, or not as impure and unholy as she knows Nora is. And then suddenly there is another, unfamiliar but strong feeling: that Nora, only Nora, can save this crazy scared person walking through the eerie night, being followed by the unnamed dead.

How did I get on this road, in the middle of nothing? she asks, looking around. She cups her gloved hands around her eyes to get a view without wind in her face. It's still dark really, miles from anything. She looks for a mysterious flash of fairylight as if it will bring with it her grandfather's voice but there is nothing here but trees, shadows, owls. Well, what did you think you'd see? a ringfort, or even an ordinary road sign saying:

Here's how Nora Cavanaugh got where she's standing:

1. she abandoned her family
2. to move 300 miles away
3. and live alone
4. and have one friend
5. who lives miles from her

6. and late one night the voices started
7. and the pictures started
8. and Nora panicked.

So, WARNING:
Don't let this happen to you.
Stay where you belong.
Do what you are supposed to, little
girls.

Is that what you thought you'd see, Nora? Did you think the town would put up a warning for wayward girls? She laughs. Girls—she is nearly thirty years old. Well, when is it safe or not a sin to disobey? She was warned not to leave. Didn't her grandmother, eighty-five and elegant, balancing on two canes, her silver hair twisted and pinned behind her beautiful head, imperious as ever, warn her about leaving home? Softened by nothing, especially her own illness which seemed to make Nonny even more remarkably determined to rule everything, Ursula Doyle had warned her granddaughter: *You don't know where you're going. You don't know anyone there. You don't know what can happen. You're being very foolish. And selfish: you'll regret this when it's too late.* Is that what had been said to the seventeen year old Ursula who had to get to Liverpool England from a small farm in the west of Ireland before she could even make the three thousand mile journey to America where none of her family had ever been? Had her mother told her, *You'll regret this when it's too late!* Had it been too late? It was a difficult send-off to be sure but given with the best of intentions. With love even. As they know it.

For Nora too. *Don't go,* warned her grandfather who, with his own penchant for impulsive travel, seldom advised against leaving home. And it hadn't been easy not to listen to him since her grandfather wasn't usually wrong about consequences. And yet this wasn't to say that her grandfather had ever managed to avoid his own difficult consequences, or the gnarled events in which he often found himself. So, why should anyone think Nora would be able to avoid the consequences of her own foolishness, whatever it was? And what in god's many names had she done that was so foolish anyway, having left home, at nearly thirty, to teach? But Nora's leaving more than worried Nonny, it angered her, though of course she never said why.

Oh, what does a town do with its wayward, furtive girls who plan and plot to leave their lots in life? Well, apparently they don't put up signs, Nora thinks, trudging on. Does no one ask these questions anymore? Do all parents expect their nearly thirty-year-old children to leave home? Not the Cavanaughs/Logans/Delaneys or Doyles. The Cavanaughs, all in Ireland, are her father's people; the Logans, all in Ireland, are her grandfather's people; Sheila, Kathleen and Eugene Delaney, the only Delaneys not in Ireland, are her first cousins, and the Doyles, mostly in Ireland, are Nonny's people. Nora, her sisters and cousins often feel like exiles. In their own country, their own homes, their own skin.

When her mother felt this way, she cleaned. Nora remembers watching her mother scrub and scrub everything in the days before she stopped cleaning, cooking, talking. One day Mary Cavanaugh seemed to have scrubbed to the layer before or beyond words and just stopped. Her grandfather sitting at their kitchen table, filling his pipe, talked about God because in those days Mary Cavanaugh was talking to everyone about God and the Church. The Catholic Church. Cleaning up the bits of tobacco Granhugh had spilled on the table, she said she wanted to find all the rules written down somewhere. "I want to see them all written down so I can look them over and try to understand something. There are some things I just don't understand. It's not that I'm questioning anything, I just have to see it written down so I can understand it. Where do you think I could find that?"

"Nowhere," Granhugh told her as Mary Cavanaugh began scrubbing Ajax into the kitchen counter. She had already scrubbed so much the blue was being bleached out of the formica. "The Church doesn't want you looking at anything written down. They don't even want you thinking about anything, written down or not. They just want you to obey. I'm not talking about Jesus Christ. Jesus didn't write down any rules and make you sign them. People forget that. They think Jesus stood whispering in the Apostles' ears while they wrote down their stories. Jesus was nowhere around. People write stories, not God. Read them if you want. They're good stories, but don't be letting the Church tell you what they mean. You know in your heart what's right. Don't let anyone tell you different."

Mary Cavanaugh wasn't too disturbed by Granhugh's talk of the Church on the days he stopped there. But sometimes he didn't. Sometimes he talked about priests and witches and the bastard English soldiers. "Didn't I see the priest threaten my father for healing people, people who needed help a doctor or priest couldn't give them? I'm not saying the priests didn't have it hard too, with bastard English soldiers hunting them, but it was the country people saved the priests, hid them, when it was putting themselves in mortal danger even to talk to a priest, so you think the priests and the Church would remember that and not be passing judgment, condemning the people's ways or calling them pagan when the priests had hold again. But the Church never tolerated any sharing. You had to believe them and nothing else or you were in sin. The Church condemned the very people who saved them. So don't be thinking your Church is so holy. Or that there's anything wrong with you just because they say so. There's nothing wrong with you that has anything to do with sin." Granhugh saw how much Nora's mother was afraid of sin. He didn't understand it, but Nora knew that he tried to comfort her mother in some way, in the way he knew: by saying there were many ways and truths in this world and you cannot condemn yourself or anyone else for finding or losing your way in any one of them. But Mary Cavanaugh couldn't feel the love in Granhugh's words. Nora watched him try over and over, whenever he visited them that summer when Nora's mother was having a baby and worried about God and sin and Satan.

The *daoine sidhe* have no buildings or priests or rules.

And no Satan. For a time in their lives Nora's mother believed Satan was persecuting her. The scary thing was she tried to fight back.

Nora remembers part of the fight. But there are parts she will never remember and she is grateful. Nora is an odd mixture of clarity and confusion—she has some of her father's fierce certainty about things (her father is usually sure about some impending tragedy, usually to take place under freak circumstances), and some of her mother's intrinsic belief that ultimately the best will happen, though not before the worst has hit them. Even if they all died in a fire, flood or family massacre, her mother believes, the best will always happen (she never elaborates on how). Nora has some of both qualities in her, alchemized by her grandfather's belief in magic, and her grandmother's very potent belief in herself.

In the woods now, the (dead) voice is gone, lost in the dark maybe. These woods are thick, not unfriendly but not tame. This could easily be a threatening place and yet to Nora these woods always seem a good place, a hiding place. Like the ancient holy burial grounds where the *daoine sidhe* gather to play the *ceol,* their music, or cast *pishogues,* fairie spells. Nora would go straight into a fairie spell now, if she could find one.

Then suddenly as if out of nowhere she knows: Eugene is dead. It wasn't a dream her mother had. Eugene is really dead. He will be nineteen in four days and he is dead. Nora is holding out her arms to be ready if she falls on the twisted trees. She thinks she can be ready.

One of Nonny's stories. That killed Eugene. That's how powerful her grandmother's stories are: they determine what you know, what you can't know. Nora, for example, though she's known some of the truth since she was ten, still almost believes that her cousins Kathleen and Sheila are twins because that's what they were always told.

Nora was with her cousins in their grandmother's basement one afternoon looking for photographs (a forbidden act made necessary by a school project) when they found some papers which weeks later the girls showed their grandfather, asking for the truth. In the basement, in the back where their grandmother kept the old furniture, Nora's cousin Kathleen climbed onto a wobbly old bureau where Nonny stored the winter/summer clothes when out of season. Even wiry little Kathleen didn't look very steady up there, reaching for the tin box hidden in the rafters. Granhugh told her to get down, to tell him what they were looking for and he'd get it, but Kath kept stretching and reaching, her dark hair falling to her waist, making her freckled arms and legs seem even paler. Kath had the only dark eyes and hair among them. Her sister Sheila had blonde hair and green eyes. And yet they believed themselves twins because that's what they had been told. We've been told, *all our lives,* Nora had felt her cousin rage that day, standing on the creaky bureau, finding evidence, of what? Lies, truth, identity, more mystery? Nora watched Kath, a thin, little, determined nine year old girl, smaller than her sister Sheila, furiously reaching to the plank above her head where her grandmother kept the big tin box full of papers and Nora knew she was seeing evidence of what mixing lies and truth can do.

They were not twins at all; they were born almost a year apart, the smaller Kath being the older sister. Granhugh admitted that much but it was too late.

Nora doesn't remember any of her grandfather's explanation because what impressed her that day was her cousin Kath's terror: *Are we sisters? Are we adopted? Am I adopted? Am I the phony one? Tell me, tell me!* Nora hadn't known that's what her cousin had been so worried and quiet about for weeks. Granhugh told them whatever he knew about birthdays, which was that Kath's came first, but he didn't know the reason for making them twins because no one thought to tell him why things were said. "But believe me, it has more to do with the ones making it up than with you." They were all still standing by the cellar door, not going up the steps to the backyard. They all knew somehow that once they went out, they would never talk about this again—not the girls with their grandfather anyway. The girls might talk among themselves, for a while, but even that would fade, each holding onto her own version but not a family version. They were too young to impose a family version of this on each other yet. But this was Nora's, what she was remembering now: her grandfather in his suit, vest, and tweed cap, standing by the cellar door with all of them, her cousin Kath saying she hated them all and wished she was adopted. "Listen, Kathleen, my girl," Granhugh said, ushering them out of the basement, "You're one of us, like it or not, no matter what stories you tell."

In the woods still, Nora thinks how hard it is to undo Nonny's stories. Especially the stories Ursula Doyle has told about herself, whoever she is. Ursula Doyle is also known as Margaret Doyle or Foley, or Clare Connelly, or Judy Perkins, or Pauline Garsen. Different names used at different times for different things: her jobs, her bank money and her (simultaneously acquired) passports. No one knows why. Or at least no one has ever divulged to Nora the motives behind the many names.

Mostly, Nora, her sisters and their cousins call their grandmother Nonny as she taught them to, not wanting to be called Grandma. (She also didn't want her husband, Hugh Logan, called Grandpa, so she tried to teach Nora, the first grandchild, to call him Hugh, while Hugh Logan was trying to get Nora to say Grandpa. Nora, trying from the first to settle family conflict, said Granhugh.)

With her many mechanical parts, having had one hip and two knee replacements, and with her quivering (though regal) posture, it would be easy to underestimate Nonny's strength and determination, but it would be dangerous. It has always been dangerous to believe appearances with Nonny. And that's a funny thing, Nora thinks, since appearance is practically all that matters to her grandmother. At least that's how it appears.

Nora was about five when she watched her mother walk around their small neat living room, smoking her cigarettes, trying to ask Nonny about things she could not remember in her own childhood. With two little girls of her own by then, Mary Cavanaugh had apparently begun to realize that there were things she'd never known about herself. She told Nonny there were just huge blank pieces she couldn't picture. Nora's mother was a painter, so pictures mattered. They mattered enough to risk asking Nonny, *Whatever happened? If you could just tell me what happened, I wouldn't have to wonder all the time and—I wouldn't feel so crazy. Can't you understand that?* Nora was only five or six, but she knew: her grandmother understood, she just didn't care. She was not going to reveal one unrevealed moment of her own life, or even her daughter's life, no matter who needed it. Even for daughter or granddaughter, Nonny would not yield, maybe because she thought she couldn't without causing more harm or hurt, but she never said that. She never said anything. Nora can still feel the chill she first felt hearing her mother's plea meet the force of her grandmother's stare.

Nora remembers her mother's warm voice: *Hold onto whatever beautiful thing you find, Norie.* On her mother's lap, Nora sat looking at the sunset, what they could see of it from their living room window. *Whatever beautiful thing you find, Norie. Hold onto it.*

But sometimes her mother couldn't hold on. She talked about the beautiful things, the light through the trees, the trees huge and black against the sky, and she said she loved these things, she wanted them, but she couldn't see them anymore. She asked Nora, still sitting in her arms, where the trees were, where the light was. "Why can't I see them, Norie? They're all gone, all those pictures. I can't see them. *Hold onto them, Norie.* There are no more brilliant beautiful things for me to find in the world," she was telling Nora, her words becoming more and more frantic, though the sound of her mother's voice, having strains of its old softness, had comforted Nora almost to the end.

The nightmare (of her mother's disintegration) had several endings. (Just like some of Nonny's stories.) At the end of the first stage, Nora's mother wasn't painting, by the end of the next stage, she wasn't talking, by the end of the end, she was gone.

"None of us had friends. That's a big part of being crazy, you know," Nora told her friend Renie one day over coffee.

"Don't be so sure you're crazy," Renie said. "You're probably remembering anything at all because you're not crazy. Don't take the easy way out."

Renie was a very practical woman, for a playwright, Nora had thought when they first met, as if Nora had known what a playwright would be like, or as if she'd ever known what practicality was, growing up in the Logan/Cavanaugh world. And yet, for all her common sense, Renie knew about voices. Well, she heard them herself, of course, as she wrote her plays, and she understood what Nora meant when she said she heard them. It took a few months before Nora would admit anything about voices because Renie had been a doctor, a psychiatrist, for years before she started writing her patients' case histories as dramas. But Renie was unlike any psychiatrist Nora had ever met, and Nora had known more than a few while taking her mother to psychiatric clinics for ten years after recovery from the breakdown. It took ten years to recover from the recovery. Nora was only beginning to write that (untold) story, beginning with the strange world of those public clinics.

Nora was about twelve when she and her mother went once a week on the bus to Queens General Hospital. If Granhugh went, he drove them, in his silver Ford Falcon, buzzing along at 80 mph, faster around bends. Nora was always relieved to have the ride, risky as it was, because her mother was afraid of buses, or really she was afraid of the people on the bus whom she thought were talking about her or taking her picture.

As they rode along, Hugh Logan always tried to talk Mary Cavanaugh out of taking any more medicine, all those tranquilizers and anti-depressants which bothered Nora too, though she didn't try to talk her mother out of taking them. In fact, it was Nora's job to dispense them. Granhugh didn't interfere with that. He didn't tell Nora that she was doing anything wrong, but she was sure that's what he was thinking: that it was Nora's fault her mother took so many pills. Nora was sure her grandfather thought that if Nora stopped giving Mary Cavanaugh all these drugs, she'd get better. But what if she didn't? What if she got as ill as she had been before? Did Granhugh ever think about that?

Another mile maybe to Renie's. Irene Kessle, doctor and well-known, remarkably prolific playwright, has been teaching for nearly fifteen years at the upstate university where Nora has been teaching for the last two years. Nora's slide into this world was based on a slim collection of stories Renie had judged for a fiction award, which Nora hadn't won, but which got her the teaching job, with Renie on the faculty hiring committee. It all seemed to happen without Nora, even the publication of the stories, many of which Nora still kept rewriting.

You could have driven these miles in half an hour, she thinks, staring at the fork in the road as if she hadn't known it would be here: the split, the choice. She needs to take the wide path to the left. The really narrow split to the right is actually closer but too broken by rocks and trees. Eventually it becomes a scraggly impassable tail of the woods behind Renie's home. Nora stands still in the eerie light. I could wander down the little path. Who would know? And then they'd only think I'd gotten lost in the snow.

You think dying will end this?

This is not any of Nora's voices. She has to stay calm, not show how afraid she is. Then she remembers: *he's dead. The person following me is dead.* Eugene? She's not sure. Why would she be afraid of Eugene?

Moving shakily down the wide road, Nora tries to recall what her mother said last night but recollects only the outline of her mother's voice and aches for the sound that was her mother's, for the mother who would come get Nora out of school, telling everyone it was a family emergency, so she could take Nora to the playground for the day or for a picnic in Alley Pond Park, or to the big movie theater on Steinway Street, or once they rode the subway all day to all the different neighborhoods in New York that her mother had lived in. They didn't get above ground once and it was quite an adventure, though Nora didn't really understand why her mother was checking each neighborhood off a list, telling as much as she could remember about the time in her life spent in each place: Sheepshead Bay, Coney Island, and Canarsie in Brooklyn, other neighborhoods in the Bronx around Van Cortland Park, a few in Manhattan, lower Manhattan, Chamber and Canal Streets, and then back to Queens. It had taken all day and it was dark by the time they got home. They never told Nora's father. And if he suspected anything, he never asked.

There were already signs of the frantic in this, of course, but still Nora remembers how wonderful and happy her mother could make things. Once her mother bought a hundred big balloons, already blown up, in all kinds of colors, with long beautiful ribbons and kept them all in the living room. "For the sheer beauty," she said. "Don't ever let anyone tell you beauty doesn't matter. You find beautiful things for yourself, Norie. And hold onto them. For yourself. You hear me?" After a while the words always became frayed. After a few days, Mary Cavanaugh said she could see the balloons dying. She said they were ill, that the air was poisoned. She told Nora's father that they couldn't live in their house anymore. Then she thought Nora's cat was the source of the poison, and Nora had to keep Logan, the cat, away from her mother. You could never be sure what Mary Cavanaugh would do as punishment or cure.

Look at what happened with the paintings. Nora will have to tell Renie about her mother's paintings. The force and passion of those pictures came out of the best in Mary Cavanaugh and were destroyed by the worst in her. It had been a time of incredible energy. Mary had been focused to the point of obsession on whatever she'd been painting. For days on end, she wouldn't cook, clean, talk even— she'd paint. The dining room was never set for a meal because the table was covered with tin cans of brushes, hundreds of brushes, some so big you could use them to paint a wall, some so small you could paint only one very fine line of color at a time as Nora sometimes watched her mother paint, and there were bottles of turpentine and oils, and raggedy spotted cloths, and sheets of paper stained with the most beautiful and unusual colors. It was unreal and yet the most real time Nora can remember. It made Nora, young as she was, want to love something in herself as much as her mother loved painting.

But it worried Nora's father—not just the mess, or that they had no meals, except whatever he boiled for himself and Nora that day. (Mary Cavanaugh smoked all the time and rarely ate anything but toast and coffee by then.) This ferocious regimen of painting worried Nora's father when he realized that she wouldn't stop because she couldn't: *something* really was wrong. That's when Ed

Cavanaugh stopped complaining to his wife and tried to pretend he didn't have to. Nora didn't understand that, but she saw that that's what her father was doing, pretending that the fifteen-hour days of painting *was* a hobby and that everything was fine. That turned out not to be a good strategy.

Nora's grandmother's strategy was to order an end to the craziness, which would have meant doing more than stopping the painting. But Nonny didn't see that. Or wouldn't see it. All she wanted was *the mess cleaned up*. That's what she ordered, unwilling to see that her daughter had become deaf to all sounds but the ones in her own head. Nonny just kept saying, "I want this mess cleaned up, Mary. Now." Almost every day, before or after work, Nonny came to their house, made herself a cup of tea, and cleaned another room as if she were showing Nora's mother how. Nora's mother paid no attention to the scrubbing and shining, and Nora watched her grandmother pay no attention to that. Nora admired the intense concentration, the focused fury of both her mother and grandmother, the complete avoidance of what each would not see. Nora felt lost, of course, standing beside but outside them both, standing somewhere inbetween their gazes. Nora was in a gully and it wasn't really safe, but at least it was out of the line of fire.

(Nora probably thinks of fire because about this time her mother started to set small but significant fires, mostly in their backyard but some were in the house. One day, Nora watched her mother gather all of her father's shoes into a neat little pyramid in the bedroom. She had lighter fluid and a few matches. That's all it took. After the shoes, the bedroom curtains and part of the bed flamed. It was a mess and smelled like smoke for a long time after that. She and Nora were able to put out the fire because they had brought the extinguisher into the bedroom before they torched the shoes. Her mother told Nora she just wanted to kill the shoes because they were talking to her. They were evil. Nora revealed that explanation to no one since she didn't think it would save her mother from all the yelling that was going on about the whole thing. For years, her father bought only one pair of shoes at a time which he either wore or kept by him, under his bed at night. Mary Cavanaugh later remarked how strange this was. Her husband certainly had become very peculiar over the years.)

It didn't take too long for Nora to figure out that she'd have to find her own place, her own intensity in this family. No one was going to give it to her, or share it with her. It wasn't a bad lesson at all.

Eventually her mother did stop painting, not because she was told to, but because, Nora came to believe, somewhere along the line of time and mind, her mother's imagination turned in on itself to see nothing as clearly as its own destruction.

Nora takes the back road up the path to Renie's house which she pictures: big, gray, gabled with black shutters and a wall of French doors. Renie's house is like Renie: confident, strong, embracing.

Nora tries to keep the house in view but she is already thinking of her grandmother's house where her cousins Kathleen and Sheila probably are now, greeting all the people who are already calling at the house to express their sorrow about their brother. Only nineteen years old—not even nineteen. Eugene won't be nineteen for another four days. What happens now? Nora wonders as if they could (or could not) possibly celebrate the birthday four days from now.

Her cousins Kathleen and Sheila, Eugene's sisters, will be in black. And so will Nora's sisters, Hallie and Tessa. All the girls, so beautiful, in black, in mourning for Eugene who will be nineteen in four days. Such a tragedy— that's what the picture will look like. Her grandmother will make sure of that. Without a brush, without a single canvas, her grandmother has painted all the pictures: the holy family, never to be as well displayed as on Sunday, every Sunday, during the Holy Communion parades, with Nora, Kath, Sheila, Tessa, Hallie in their starched Sunday dresses and for a while even Eugene in his navy blue suit and shined shoes, all following their beautiful grandmother to the altar at Mass, as if they didn't already know it was the picture of the pretty, well-behaved children with their grandmother that mattered. Nora knew and didn't care. She wanted to be that pretty, well-behaved granddaughter who could make her grandmother proud. She wanted even to be the picture of that granddaughter, if it would make her grandmother proud. Even now she would be that picture. She doesn't care that the picture matters more than the truth, which Nora doesn't know anyway.

Some of the truth is that Eugene—blonde and beautiful—is lying in his coffin. Try to make a proud picture of that, she thinks, pushing along. But there will be a picture, a story. It's probably already being told to Kathleen, to Sheila, to Sheila's children (to save for their children).

Suddenly Nora pictures her cousin Sheila with her blonde hair twisted somehow onto the top of her head, never with a pin or barrette or anything. Sheila just seems to tie it there, where it stays, except for the pieces falling alongside her bangs which fall down to her big green eyes. Nora remembers Sheila standing in the middle of her livingroom, surrounded by toys. She had two babies then. Was that the last time Nora saw her? It couldn't have been, but it is the most vivid picture Nora has of her: Sheila in jeans and an old shirt, her hair twisted on her head, toys in her hand, telling someone to do something. She was making a world for herself, with her husband, her kids. She was making a good place. Nora wasn't sure how she was doing it, by sheer determination and some idea of what she was doing, by some picture of herself doing it. She was making a world and she kept doing it, never at all saying such a thing, or able to hear it said. She is like Nora's tough talky sister Tessa (who's had a much harder time finding the sane seam to follow in what she's designing for herself) but neither will talk about or admit anything really, though they won't deny anything Nora or Kathleen say. About their lives. This is all about their lives. What it has been: they are still piecing that together. How they have lived it: they are still piecing that together too, going carefully around the edges which are surprisingly sharp. Like ice through the trees. Or glass splintered on the floor.

All you have is family, their grandmother (who left all the family she'd ever known) warned these four little girls often enough when they were growing up so that none of them should be questioning it now. *Family is all you have. If you do not have family, you have nothing.* They were told to trust no one else. When eighteen year old Sheila Delaney said she was marrying Nick Palmieri, she was told, *No.* Being Sheila Delaney and unafraid, she said, "Yes, I'm marrying with or without any of you." Nonny warned that Sheila would be sorry, she would see what leaving her family, what mixing with other people would bring. *Italians! what do you know about them?*

Sitting at the kitchen table that day, her hands folded, Nora offered that the Pope was Italian. Nonny's slow serious gaze found Nora. "The Pope," she told them, "doesn't marry."

"Not because he's Italian," Nora said before she was told to leave. And did. Sheila needed no help; she stood her ground, but each sister and cousin stood with her.

You girls have each other. And they knew they were lucky for it. They didn't know yet to argue that was a beginning and not an end. Mostly they didn't argue; they made their decisions and lived them as hard as it was. As they'd been taught: *I came here with nothing, knowing no one. Don't be telling me how hard your life is.*

To her daughters and granddaughters, Ursula Doyle seemed invincible, and capable of anything. And she was.

*

Eugene will be nineteen, in only four days, and he's dead. That's how hard his life has been, Nora thinks, walking to Renie's house, for some reason remembering the morning she went to the hospital to see her cousin the day after Sheila's daughter had been born. Going into the room, Nora saw her cousin lying in bed, seeming asleep but not looking rested, in fact looking as if some huge human struggle were still going on when Nora realized that Sheila was crying, without a sound, her eyes closed. Nora waited for her to stop. She knew that in a second, Sheila would open her eyes and say something funny so they could both deny this moment, but for once Sheila didn't. She opened her eyes, saw Nora, and asked, still crying, "What have I done?"

It took Sheila more than a week to name the baby, and then finally, against her mother's and grandmother's wishes (what will people think *that* name means?), Sheila with a desperate, urgent fury named her daughter Hope.

Pictures pressing, burning in the cold, Nora is nearly at the house. *Even the house seems tired.* That's what Kathleen said once, sounding tired herself. She'd been telling Nora about her brother Eugene coming home from jail. He'd been home only a few days. It was summer. Nora was with Kathleen in the back yard of their grandmother's house. They were sitting on the glider, drinking ice tea, having headaches from the sun, Kath curling her long dark hair away from her neck, saying that she was going to marry Tony—Nick Palmieri's brother. Nick and Sheila were only married about a year, and no one even realized that Kathleen and Nick's brother Tony knew each other. No one knew about this but Sheila and now Nora. It was important that no one know till Kath was ready to tell her mother and grandmother. It would be another battle, like the one over Sheila's engagement to Nick, *the Italian boy. Marry your own kind,* Nonny told Sheila, who laughed though she knew how deadly serious this could be. *Your own kind!* was a battle cry, a declaration of family against family. But Sheila Delaney laughed because that was her weapon: to say there would be no war. She had already won, she was the one born here. *We're both Americans*, she told their grandmother. *You're the only foreigner here. If that's the word you want to use, use it on yourself.* And what could Nonny say? Her granddaughter had betrayed her, had turned the family inside out, exposing them all to dangers they couldn't even imagine yet. That's what Nonny told Sheila who married Nick Palmieri in a small ceremony at her friend Debbie's house, with her cousins and Nora's parents there, Nora's father walking Sheila down the staircase. (It was after this that the gambling stories started about Ed Cavanaugh.) But Sheila had her day, her wedding day. She was sure about herself, and Nick. And Kath was sure about Tony, but not as set in herself. Kath could be hurt by her mother and grandmother. She still wanted their affection. And that, Nora knew, could get you killed.

So, that summer day, just after Eugene had come home from jail, Kath was telling Nora that she was going to marry Tony as soon as she got out of nursing school. She'd be working and Tony was a musician and making some money, so they would be fine. "Even if we don't have a cent, it'll be better than this," Kath said, still holding her thick dark hair away from her neck to get a breeze. "And then it will be just Eugene in the house with them." With her mother and grandparents. "They'll probably kill each other. It's bad already and he's only been home a few days. Even the house can't take it anymore," Kath said in her own dispassionate way that they all had from their grandmother. But Kathleen's practical manner was not as accomplished as her sister Sheila's. Kathleen's composure was mixed with a very taut anxiety so that she seemed neither touched nor untouched by the things that were deeply upsetting her.

That day it had been that Eugene and their mother were already fighting. (Peg had to do her own fighting with her son since she had no husband to do it for her. Gil Delaney, her children's father, had been dead for years, and Peg's short marriage to Arthur Crowley was already over.) Kath seemed very tired as she told Nora, "Eugene doesn't hit her but he put a hole in the kitchen wall behind the door and he ripped out the light from above the kitchen sink." Kathleen hadn't said much more, just that even the house was bruised now. This was their grandmother's house. Kathleen and Sheila and Eugene grew up there, with their parents, in their grandparent's house. Their mother had moved back to this house, to her mother, taking her husband Gil with her, three months after her wedding. No one said why.

Even the house seems tired. That's as much as Kathleen could say about the relentless emotion and exhaustion of their lives. You could feel it in the timber of the house. You could hear it reflected in the uncertainty of their voices, as if their own sounds were about to break with all the unmentioned strain. Nora only knew the little she knew of Eugene from what Kath or Sheila told her when they couldn't hold it in anymore. But even with only a few clues: the dropping out of school, the running away, the stolen cars, the missing money, the fighting, the calls at night from the police, the calls at night *to* the police—it was a relentless story, and yet never quite there.

> *Don't trust the dead*
> *Or many of the living*
> *Everything changes*
> *Nothing changes*
> *Never be quite sure*
> *Don't doubt yourself*
> *Always sit by a window*
> *Keep a candle in your pocket*

Voices.

Nora carries these voices into Renie's house, into the sunlit hall, words running wild inside her now: split in glass, blood in snow, a sharp blade or breath down her throat. All crazy. She has to slow them, the words and pictures. In the front hall of Renie's house, shaking off cold and snow, she puts her hat on the cherrywood chair by the door, and slowly removes her gloves. Her hands are raw. Slowly, she steps into the sunlight that is shooting everywhere in the front hall. Looking up, as if the sun is coming through the roof, Nora takes a breath and calls, "Renie?" Nora can barely hear herself. She doesn't want to cry, and that knot of unwanted sound is stuck in the middle of her throat, cutting off any other sound. Eyes down, her arms limp at her side, she tries again in a whisper to herself, "Renie?"

Pulling her heavy black coat around her, shivering against the wetness, Nora walks a few feet to the tall oak staircase that goes up to the second and then turns a bit to go to the little landing at the top of the third floor. She looks up as she sits on the bottom stairs, in the sun, waiting, for whatever has happened to begin.

II. *The Honeysuckle Sweet Funeral And the World Behind It*

𝕹𝖔𝖗𝖆 walks through the archway to her left into the huge living room and sits in the nearest chair, looking at the polished parquet floor, noticing her soaked boots. She has no energy to remove them. She can spare nothing from the effort to keep from being swept into the storm of this story. Whatever strength she has is already spilling into thoughts of how she will tell this, whatever has happened, to Renie who will want it told clearly from the beginning, as if there is a beginning. "Well, Renie, something began when I talked to my mother last night. I fell deep into my grandmother's web. Deadcenter. Oh, yeah—the dead are everywhere. Not only my cousin. Did I tell you Eugene is dead? If someone in our family dies, my grandmother has something to do with it, or at least with the story. Believe me, Renie, if we ever get to the heart of this thing, my grandmother will be there, waiting for us, smiling, offering us a cup of tea. Don't drink it. I'll tell you why later."

Nora stops, sensing this is not very clear. "Maybe I should start with some introductions," she says, wishing

Renie were here to stop her from this rambling. "I'll start with my grandparents: Hugh Logan and Ursula Doyle. They are exceptional people. My grandfather has mystical Celtic powers and my grandmother has great herbal knowledge. They're very gifted. Yes, that's the place to start. Or maybe I should just start with how they met: through Ursula's brother Laurence Doyle, the bootlegger, or maybe I should tell why Hugh and Ursula married: for the house, or why they stayed together, except I don't have the answer to that yet."

Noticing the phone on the table by the sofa, Nora considers getting up from her comfortable chair and calling her sister Hallie. The last time they talked, Hallie told Nora about visiting Granhugh while he was recovering from his heart aneurysm that hadn't really burst on him because he'd checked himself into Queens General Hospital just in time. He was out of danger by the time Hallie saw him crawling under his bed to find his extra pair of teeth. "If you leave anything where you can't see it in this hospital it's gone." The teeth weren't even his. He'd found them on the nightstand by the bed when he woke up from his operation. They were a good enough fit for a spare set, he told Hallie, and he didn't want to lose them.

"Nora?"

Renie is standing in front of her, waiting as if Nora will explain the cold wet coat or the mix of panic and pain Nora knows she hasn't kept from crossing her face. Nora stays in her chair and stares up, as if caught, cornered.

"Where the hell have you been?"

"I walked—" Nora gets up, going across the room to the French doors as if to show Renie how she walked.

"For three days? You've been walking out there for three days? I've been calling everywhere. What happened?"

"Nothing." Nora sits back down in the tapestry wing chair to pull off her boots, snow and ice melting everywhere on the floor and carpet. "I'm sorry," she says, meaning that she is sorry about the mess of snow. She doesn't know what else she's done.

Renie takes the coat, sweater and boots across the room to the hall closet while Nora opens her blouse, not wanting to look at her left side. She knows that just under her breast is a deep bruise, probably even deeper than she remembers from last night. It is an enormous thing that has happened and Nora can't remember it.

Except: she knows something from the pain, she can almost feel something of the moment just before whatever happened: she remembers bracing herself. That's all: bracing herself for the blow.

She buttons her blouse.

Be still, her mother used to say when the panic was rising. Nora came to see that her mother meant *be still* inside yourself, calm yourself, talk to yourself, take yourself out of whatever is frightening you. Nora has to anchor herself now. She has to be still and calm but not drift too far from where she is. Renie is still a doctor. Nora has to be careful.

She looks around, naming each thing she sees in the room, keeping herself fixed to this place and time. "Books, two walls of books, Renie's books on the tables," Nora says, turning her head, seeing more books on the library table to the left of her just behind the dark blue sofa with the wooden legs and curved back; the other plump paisley sofa is across the room from her, against the wall to the left when you come in the room from the archway in the front hall. "Renie went through there to the closet," she reminds herself. She looks to the fireplace ahead of her. There is a fire going. Renie's been home? She's been waiting for me? For three days? I've been gone three days? How could I be gone three days?

On the mantelpiece are the photographs of Renie's family. Her daughter Emma, and husband Malcolm. Nora met Emma once. She seemed a lot like Renie: very smart, direct, sure of herself. Emma hadn't liked Nora. For the wrong reasons, Nora thinks. Between the paisley sofa and the other tapestry wing chair (Renie usually sits in) by the fire is the big, square, oak coffee table. In the middle of it sits a vase of flowers—pale roses with sprigs of baby's breath. Renie always has flowers, even in winter. They are beautiful but Nora can't look at them. She turns her head right and looks out the windowed doors to the field of snow. "I should just walk right into the stretch of whiteness."

"Don't even think about it," Renie warns, coming back in the room and standing in front of Nora.

"I tried to call you last night—" Nora begins.

"You've been gone three days, Nora. You never called, you never tried to call. I've been here."

"My mother called *last night*," Nora insists, watching Renie stand by the windows. "I should call her. I think I said I would call her. That must be what I said." Nora wants to say that she has to call Kathleen and Sheila. But she can't think how to explain any of this yet.

"You're shivering. Why don't you sit on the sofa, by the fire," Renie says, sounding softer, moving towards Nora.

Listen Renie, Nora wants to tell her but she is suddenly afraid to hear her own voice. She's afraid it won't be her own. *Listen,* Renie, she wants to warn: these words won't always be my own. And I won't always know that. But Nora says nothing, sitting on the paisley sofa by the far wall.

Renie puts more wood on the fire, before going upstairs, telling Nora she'll be right back.

It doesn't matter, Nora thinks, as she sits with her hands folded on her knees on the edge of the plump sofa by the fire, wondering if all this were *pishogues,* fairie spells, like Granhugh used to tell her about. None of this is real, she thinks, her head pounding as she falls back on the sofa, remembering Sunday dinners of all things: her family gathered around her grandmother's table, the mashed potatoes and well-done roast beef being passed around, the gravy spilling on the white, ironed, Irish linen, the talk going on without a sign of trouble when without warning, her slightly drunk grandfather stands up and accuses their grandmother of having lied to him about something. Once he accused her of having lied to him about everything, his whole life. "My whole life, old woman."

Still eating, Nonny told him, "I haven't even known you your whole life, Hugh Logan."

"You've known enough of it to have sucked most of the good out of it, haven't you?" Granhugh whipped back at her, standing there at the head of the table, everyone quiet, Nonny still eating as Nora and her sister Tessa and their cousins, around eight or nine then, and the babies Hallie and Eugene around three, watched, trying to gauge how much of an argument this would be—would they ever get to tea and cake? It depended on how Granhugh took Nonny's silence, and that depended on how she said or even didn't say anything now. Nonny's silences always seemed the same to Nora, but they weren't, and Granhugh could detect how they weren't. Nora watched Granhugh: a small, wiry man, with wild white hair and very quick eyes. He wore suspenders and a belt, a vest and sweater, and his neck looked as slender as a broomstick even in the smallest of dress shirts. His clothes overwhelmed him, and yet his voice was big, round—blasting from the pit of him, as he'd ask, "You hear me, old woman? I'm tired of you thinking you can do anything you like. Don't think I don't know what you're doing."

Silence.

"Don't think I don't know!"

"You're mad," Nonny said quietly, finishing her meal.

"Mad am I? Tell me you haven't been saying nothing to these children about me. You'd think I was just a visitor in this house for all anyone knows about me."

His (step)daughters, granddaughters and grandson stared at him, knowing it was true. They knew things about him but there was a way in which they'd been kept from knowing him and they didn't even know what it was.

"What am I supposed to say about you, Hugh Logan?" Nonny asked, her back straight, not at all disheveled. Nothing shook her, ever. She pushed the last of the mashed potatoes on her fork with her knife, and said, sounding very tired of this whole business of Granhugh's, "You're talking nothing but your own foolishness. And I don't know why you think anyone wants to hear it."

"I don't give a damn what any of you want!" Granhugh shouted. That's when he lost. Nonny was always calm and above his sound. As soon as he yelled, she won. Nora didn't know why, but she saw it, sitting at that dinner table every Sunday. And they saw some version of this nearly every Sunday. Even before they knew what any of the accusations and denials were about, the daughters, granddaughters and grandson knew that they were witnesses and players in a continuous story that they were taking into their bones, not always knowing the meaning but living by it. Every Sunday, Nora, her sisters and cousins sat in a row down from their grandmother who sat at their grandfather's side, eating her dinner as their grandfather stood at the head of the table, accusing and pleading, Nora wanting him to say, *I'm not a fool and you know it. I've given a big part of my life to you and you've accepted that, even if you won't admit or acknowledge it. You've taken it, and it hasn't been for nothing!* But he never said this. All Hugh Logan ever said was, "None of you better sleep too soundly tonight because I'm mad enough to kill you all in your beds."

No one replied. Well, what could they say?

Taking the nightgown, robe, and socks Renie hands her, Nora unbuttons her wet blouse and hesitates.

"I'll get us some tea," Renie says, sensing Nora's discomfort, offering to leave her alone.

"No." Nora surprises herself, though she is still unable to move, or explain.

"What's the matter?" Renie waits.

Nora moves her blouse off her left shoulder, unable yet to look at the awful blue mottled skin. For the first time, she touches the bruise, feeling a hot ache spread across her side. "It hurts," is all she says.

Renie kneels by the sofa. "Move your hand. Let me see, please." Renie moves Nora's hand away. "What hurts?"

Nora looks. "It was all bruised—I fell, I think. I fell or I was hit and fell—" But Nora sees no mark where there had been deep bruises, where she has been bruised for days, or longer.

"What happened?" Renie asks, still kneeling by Nora, not upset.

"I don't know." This unnerves Nora. All she has to rely on is what she sees. It is bad enough, frightening enough not to remember things, important things, to have huge blank holes where memories should be, but it feels worse, more frightening to have memories or thoughts that aren't true. I was bruised, she thinks, saying nothing.

"It's all right," Renie says as if she believes it. "You're exhausted. Put the nightgown on and lie down there," she tells Nora, going away again.

But Nora sits, not putting on the nightgown, not moving, not even trying to untangle what she knows or doesn't know. She is stunned. She looks around the room again to be sure she hasn't imagined everything. How can she be sure? *Never believe only what you see.* Granhugh's voice. But can I believe what I don't see?

"Here," Renie says as she comes in with a blanket and begins to help Nora into the nightgown, robe and socks, moving like a mother getting a child ready for bed as Nora lets her, wondering if these comforting motions are real or not. Done, Renie sits in the chair by the fire while Nora wraps the blanket around herself. "I'm fine." She leans back, her long red hair wet against her neck as her head rests on the back of the sofa.

"Oh, you're fine. You're out there for days while I think you're dead. What did you think you were doing?"

"I thought I was running away," Nora says.

"Running away from what?"

"I don't know. From what happened, or what was going to happen—" Without warning, Nora thinks of her Aunt Peg's bluing face, how the blood broke beneath the skin of Peg's right cheek and discolored that side of her face, the bruise spreading just below her chin. It was a stunning thing, the bruise and the blow, neither of which anyone ever mentioned. Not even Kathleen who, Nora is sure, had seen her mother struck.

"What happened?" Renie asks.

Nora thinks of Peg but then realizes that was almost twenty years ago. "What happened last night? My mother called—" And then Nora remembers: "My cousin's dead—"

"Kathleen?" Renie asks, obviously stunned. Kathleen is the cousin Nora usually mentions.

Nora is startled too. "No, her brother, Eugene."

"Eugene?"

"Kathleen and Sheila's younger brother. He'll be nineteen in four days."

"How did he die?"

"What?"

"What happened to him?"

This also startles Nora, as if Renie should know this, as if everyone already knows this. "He was killed."

"How?"

"An accident." These questions don't answer anything. *How did he die? My grandmother's story*. That's the answer, Nora thinks, afraid of what else she knows: there were drops of blood in the snow. She saw Eugene fighting someone in the back of her grandmother's house. When was that? Nora is afraid to tell about seeing that because she knows some part of it is her fault and some other part of it couldn't have happened. She's already told Renie about the bruise that isn't there.

"It's awful news," Renie says, "but why did you run?"

"I panicked."

"Well, I know, but why?"

"I don't know. It was just awful. I ran."

"Why didn't you take the car?"

"I just started to run. I didn't think. Don't ask me any more."

Renie laughs. "I've just begun."

Nora closes her eyes.

"All right, rest now. And don't worry: you're not crazy, you're exhausted. That's all. Three days out in this weather's enough to wipe out most of anyone's mind. Temporarily."

Nora understands the warning: She will have to talk, and feeling safe for the moment from scrutiny as Renie goes to the kitchen, she thinks she will talk, in a few hours, or a few days. But not now. Now she wants the questions to stop. And for a moment she thinks they have, till one circles and demands, *How did he die?*

An accident. Nora sees: Eugene laughing and then something happens and Eugene's head goes back with a laugh that seems to stitch his side the way some laughs do, and Eugene puts his hand to the place where the laugh catches him because by now, a second later, there is some awful pain that contorts his face and surprises him with the realization that he is about to die, because he realizes that with this kind of pain it can happen. In a second. The way huge irrevocable things do. In a second. He is just so surprised and then not surprised at all. He's been expecting this, he says, 'Oh, I knew it,' he says, as if pleased with himself.

Curled on the sofa, warm in the blanket, Nora feels sleep surround her. And in a moment she is taken into a thick full sleep so complete that breathing and sleep seem all there is in a world collapsed into nothing but this moment:

She is at the funeral home, standing next to her elegant grandmother at the open coffin, greeting people, taking their hands, talking quietly as if death really were a sleep you could disturb. Nonny stands there for hours, though she's not supposed to be standing for hours like this on her fake joints. But *she's so strong. She never complains.* Each girl takes a turn standing with her beautiful, imperious grandmother, believing how strong she is. Except Tessa. They can't find Tessa. That tough little talky Tessa doesn't care what anyone thinks or says. She's not standing there to be a pretty picture for people she doesn't even know, who didn't even know Eugene or anything that happened. That's what Tessa says. And though it is Nora who is asked to ask Tessa to take her turn at their grandmother's side, Nora admires her sister's resistance, and clarity. Tessa is right—about the picture at least: the girls are meant to be pretty pictures to belie the horrific picture of beautiful but lost Eugene lying in his coffin. They know this as well as Tessa does, but they disguise their grandmother's intentions from themselves because if they know, as clearly as Tessa does, that they are *meant* to be pictures, that they are really nothing to their grandmother *but* pictures, they, like Tessa, would have to refuse, almost anything to do with her. And they don't. That's what amazes Nora: not their grandmother's strength, but their own.

Nora sits up, touching her eyes for a moment, feeling something, the light hurt. Her throat burns.

Renie puts her book down. "You slept a few hours," she says, moving to the square oak table to pour tea. Nora watches, urgently, hanging onto particular movements as if something in ordinary motion, in the ordinary itself can somehow heal her.

Renie puts the teacup and saucer on the table by Nora and pours herself a cup. "I have this tea set a long time," she tells Nora, "and I like it but seldom allow myself to use it." She is sitting in her chair again by the fire. One leg curled under the other, Renie sits back, cup in one hand, saucer in the other.

Nora isn't drawn to Renie's considerable fame, though Nora supposes that's what people think. It's not what Renie thinks. Nora knows that Renie is curious about her, about anyone who can detect her own well-buried qualities, the caring most people don't see in Renie who can be very abrupt and almost always intimidating in her breadth of knowledge, as well as in her reputation and manner.

"Allow yourself?" Nora asks, hearing her own words as if they've been said by someone else, very far away. By her very controlled and composed grandmother.

"This was my sister's tea set," Renie explains. "My sister died more than twenty years ago, and it hurts to think that all her beautiful things are still here and she's gone, forever."

"Well, you're right to put away the tea set and never use it." Nora pulls the blankets up to her shoulders. She is cold. "Things hurt less if you lock them up, never go near them."

"You know better than that."

"I don't know a thing," Nora says, suddenly afraid that she is near the edge of wanting to hurt Renie.

"People think they're strong if they don't talk about what hurts them. But it's not the talking that will kill you. You know better," Renie says again.

"I'm just tired of the dreams, that's all." Nora's voice sounds nearer but still strange to her. She hasn't reached for the tea. She doesn't know what is going to happen here. Has she told Renie about Eugene's accident? That's what she wants to ask as she hears herself saying, "Your sister would want you to have the pleasure of this fine tea set."

"My sister haunts me. And when she visits, it's not pleasure she brings."

"She comes here? You see her?"

"Yes."

"She wants to hurt you?"

"No. She wants to stop herself from being hurt. After being dead more than twenty years, it's enough pain."

"What does she want you to do?"

"It's a long story. Let's just say I can't do what she wants. And so, you see, it doesn't seem right to use her tea set."

"But you do."

"Yes. Because I'm alive, and I can. You see?"

"Yes." Renie is telling Nora not to let the dead have more power than the living. Renie already knows Nora's night of wandering has something to do with the dead.

"Good," Renie says. "I know it all seems—"

"It feels as though everything—everything I know, everything I am is breaking," Nora says, thinking, *Like glass all over the floor.* "It's all breaking, Renie," Nora says to cover the sounds beginning in her. "So easily. You don't even realize what's happening and it's all shattered in pieces on the floor, and you think: No, wait, it's a mistake, an accident. I didn't mean to do it. I'm sorry. But no one listens, and the pieces are there, cutting you if you're not careful. You see?"

"Yes."

Nora is very near to crying. And Kathleen and Sheila? Nora pictures the wake as if she's already seen it, as if she's already been there. Kathleen—small and lovely in her black linen, tight-waisted dress. A summer dress, in the middle of winter? Well, just pictures. Kathleen does cry at the funeral, or will cry, though she will ask Nora not to tell anyone. Only Nora will see her.

"Things get broken inside so easily, Renie."

"People are really stronger than that," Renie says quietly, drinking her tea.

"Some people. But for some people it's too hard. It's too much. Look at Emma." Renie's daughter Emma has been fighting leukemia for almost a year now. Nora *is* going to hurt Renie. To make her understand this. Nora wants her to feel, as if Renie hasn't already felt, what it is to have something happen, something you can't change, that changes everything forever. Emma changes everything. Eugene, dead, changes everything, forever. Laughing one second and then dead in the next. Deadcenter. In the spiderweb of stories whose sticky seductive threads they are all too afraid to tear down and see behind. Nora wants someone to understand this.

"Emma hasn't given up," Renie says.

"Yes," says Nora. "I'm sorry."

"For what?"

Bringing her arm from under the blanket, Nora reaches over to where the cup and saucer sit on the table, running a finger round the rim of the pale blue china. How can Renie be kind to her? How can Renie think she deserves kindness? Renie will find out. "For saying what I shouldn't."

"What shouldn't you say?"

"How's Emma?" Nora asks, not surprised by her own cruelty.

"I don't know," Renie says, hiding her hurt if she feels it—because of her daughter Emma or because of Nora. For months at a time, Emma lets no one near her but a few friends, and her father. Not Renie. "Did you know that my sister who died was named Emma?" Renie asks, telling the story she doesn't want to tell, hoping this will let Nora tell hers.

Nora knows this is what Renie is doing, and Nora sees too that this is generous of Renie, this is more than Nora deserves.

"Your daughter is named for your sister?"

"Emma was born while my sister was ill, while she was dying. We all knew that my sister was going to die, but we didn't say that to each other, or to her. My other sisters and I were all in our twenties, and even with Emma's death staring us in the face—she wore it on her face, we couldn't believe it. I was at Johns Hopkins, at med school, for God's sake, and I couldn't face what was happening.

So we left her alone with that, because we were afraid. Afraid that if we said it, it would happen. And maybe even happen to us. And now it's happening to my daughter. Sometimes I wake in the dead of night and think my sister Emma is coming to claim my daughter, and she's the one I'm furious with, still—my poor dead sister. And she says to me, in the dead of night, 'Didn't you give her to me? to appease me for what you were doing? Didn't you give her to me, didn't you, Irene?'

"And I admit, 'Yes, I did, Em, but not now, not when she is so young, with so much life to go—' And my dead sister tells me, 'But that's when you gave her to me. She's mine.' And I scream at her, sometimes in a dream, sometimes sitting at the kitchen table at three in the morning. I scream at my sister to help Emma, to help me, as if she can, as if I deserve it."

Nora keeps her look to Renie's dark green eyes, wanting but not wanting Renie to ask what she finally does ask, "What really happened to Eugene?"

Shakily, Nora reaches for her tea as Renie tells her, "The only things that are falling apart are your coping mechanisms, my dear, the ways you've been able to keep yourself from feeling *anything* all these years."

Nora only knows, "You couldn't help your family and I can't help mine."

"What's happened is awful but you haven't done it, and it's not you who has to help everyone through it."

Renie thinks Nora means Eugene's death, but Nora realizes that's not what happened, not last night anyway.

*

As if she has already lived through this, Nora sees herself standing by her cousin's casket. She is with Kathleen, touching Kathleen's shoulder as if that can be comfort enough. They don't look at Eugene. They can't bear it. Or believe it? They can't believe it.

Eugene is very young, and strong—more than six feet and muscular. His hands and neck are big. And yet, in some ways he looks like a child, with his curly blonde hair and those iceblue eyes that are closed now forever but which used to turn from ice to fire so quickly that you knew immediately when he didn't understand something, or when he was embarrassed and ashamed that he didn't understand, ashamed of himself—like a child. But a dangerous child. A child who by the age of six terrifies his mother with the cruelty he possesses and which possesses him, for it is uncontrolled and, his mother sees (though most of the time denies to herself) this cruelty is already uncontrollable. Already stronger in the son than in the father (and husband) whose cruelty was always tempered by a cowardice Eugene Delaney never possessed. Never. Even at the end, the cowardice is not Eugene's. Or the lies. For as Nora stands with her cousin Kathleen by the casket they will not look in because then they would know that what they all want to think (that this death is a final peace for Eugene who suffered so much since he was a child) is a lie, another lie.

"How did he die?"

"Protecting his girlfriend from an insult," Nora hears Aunt Peg say later that afternoon at the wake, with a perfect pitch—somewhere between disbelief and grief. *He was like that you know, a good boy. He never had a chance.* (It's a story they tell so well that the sadness (which is real) mixes with something sweet (which is unreal) till you wonder what it is you taste in your mouth, for a second thinking it's honeysuckle, it's so sweet and odd a taste, something you are not supposed to taste, and then you know the mix of real and unreal isn't sweet at all, it's cold, metal—the taste of tin, and then you know: it's fear you have in your mouth; then you wonder what world is this you're in and can't get out of without dying?)

Nora is tempted to stand by her aunt and ask, "Where is she, this girlfriend whose life has been saved?" Nora is tempted to ask as if it will somehow defend Eugene's honor as if honor is truth, as if how he died is the only truth to be told about Eugene. But Nora never protected him or his honor in life. What right does she have to it now?

Nora remembers wanting to comfort Kathleen as only she and Nora stand by Eugene's casket. She remembers what hasn't happened yet? Or will happen again because events in their lives go round and round, unending, unchanged for generations? How did they become such people?

She remembers that she does nothing but put a hand to her cousin's shoulder, thinking: Kathleen probably thinks I mean to stop her, to tell her to get hold of herself. "Don't tell anyone," Kathleen asks Nora, ashamed of her weakness. They are all so ashamed of themselves. You can taste it.

III. Memory, Night
And Candles

𝕿elltelltelltelltell—Nora wakes
up running the word at herself as if it were a round of
bullets, not knowing what to tell if she could. She takes a
breath and swings her legs off the sofa, intending to stand,
realizing she can't. She feels sore and reaches for the bruise
that isn't there just under her left arm. A stunning thing.
There or not. As startling as the glass falling. For the first
time Nora connects the glass falling with the bruise. As if
it is happening again she remembers: a glass shattering on
the floor in a dark room. Stopping there, it begins again,
memory rippling; words, and now pictures splinter into
echoes somehow coming together. After having been flung
away years ago as far away as Nora could send them, these
memories are on their way back, with the power of a mount-
ing return.

She sits on the edge of the sofa, bent over, in her nightgown and robe, staring at the thick pale yellow socks she
has on her feet. She feels shaky—from remembering the
glass she broke in her grandmother's house one afternoon

when she should have been more careful; if she had only been careful and quiet, nothing would have happened.

Where's Renie, she thinks, wanting nothing to do with the memory of her grandmother's house, only now remembering that the phone rang a while ago and Renie went into her study to answer it. Maybe she's talking to a doctor or the hospital. After all, Renie's still a doctor. She could give me an injection and send me to Paris for about a year. But I can't paint, Nora thinks, in her own defense. She knows she'll need a defense. Her mother didn't have one. That's how she ended up in Paris, in Nonny's story. They are all in one of Nonny's stories.

Nora pulls the blanket over her shoulders as something—the memory she does not want—creeps into the center of her rest, standing over her as she tries to sleep. A cold chill goes down her throat. She is very still.

She hears the words breathed into her ear, *Move and I'll make it hurt more.* She is eleven years old.

Nora has to be very still. That's the only part she remembers. It's more than she wants to remember, even now, almost twenty years later. But even twenty years later, she is very still. And blank. For minutes. Even remembering nothing of this but the familiar coming out of that blankness, pulling herself out of that cool deep dead place where she hides, Nora knows that the wrong word or sound or move can get her killed. This is uncontrollable except by stillness and silence. She knows this as she knew it then when she was eleven. In her grandmother's house.

As quickly as reflex, she pulls good memories: her grandfather mixing his tobacco on his living room floor, the newspapers spread and filled with the different blends, as Nora and Kathleen, only about four or five, help him. They put their hands through the mound of brown flakes. They have its smell on their hands for days after. "Do that in the garage," Nonny tells Granhugh, not wanting the tobacco to stain her carpet. He says he'll mix his tobacco any damn place he wants. He says this after Nonny leaves, and they always finish before she comes home. Nora and Kathleen never tell, and they never tell about smoking his pipe. Granhugh shows them how: to take little sips of breath first, till they get used to the taste, and then to inhale slowly and let the taste go down and out. It takes a while to learn. Granhugh tells them that most country people smoke the pipe in Ireland, men and women. His mother and father and neighbors spent many an evening round the turf fire, sharing tobacco; it's important to smoke on certain occasions too, especially weddings and wakes. At either there's always a basket of clay pipes, one for everyone; the tobacco is handed around and the pipes lit. Tobacco is a plant the devil can't abide, you see, Granhugh tells them, so it's smoked to keep you safe. The souls of the dead can find a safe passage to heaven on the smoke of all the funeral pipes. It's important to smoke the pipe at a wake, Granhugh tells them. Nora has to remember this.

And also: *You can't always trust the dead.*

What kind of crazy family am I part of, she wonders, when you have to worry about the living and dead? When the dead don't stay dead? This is a lot of trouble, keeping track of who's back and who's not. Just keeping track of who's who is a lot of work in this family. There are so many people for the same part, it's exhausting. Not to mention the different names people use.

Nora was about eight or nine when she realized that her grandmother had a few names. When any of her grandchildren called her at work, at the hospital for instance, they never asked for Ursula Doyle but Margaret Foley. Nora and Kathleen never questioned why. In fact, for a long time, Kathleen and Nora thought you got to make up a new name for yourself when you got a job. They didn't realize till much later that years ago Nonny had needed several names for several jobs because she was also collecting *assistance* for her fatherless children who would have had no food in the Great Depression (and years afterward) if their mother had had only one name.

And then in time, the names had to do with other things. One, for instance, had something to do with a bank vault which wasn't their grandmother's, of course, but belonged to Nonny's (dead) brother's wife. Nonny hadn't even known her brother Laurence had had a wife till after he was dead and the wife showed up to get his clothes. Laurence didn't leave much more, and from the looks of her, Granhugh said, the wife didn't have much more either. "Probably going to pawn the clothes." Nonny was furious, at the wife she didn't even know and not at the brother it turned out she didn't know either, the brother who had lied about a great deal more than a wife. When Nonny went through the papers Laurence had left in his room (papers that the wife, not knowing about, hadn't asked for), Nonny found the wife's name, a marriage certificate, and something about a bank vault. Nonny said the marriage meant nothing. It hadn't been in Church. Granhugh said it meant enough to be causing all this trouble and she better call the wife about the papers if Nonny ever wanted to get into the vault and find out what was there. But Nonny had no intention of calling the wife. She didn't need the wife to get into the vault. Nonny already had what she needed of the wife: she had her name, Pauline Garsen, and Nonny, of course, used it.

That's just what Nonny always did: cut and patched things, events, people, so well you couldn't even see the seams most of the time. And sometimes, Nora admits, it was a good thing. Once her grandmother had been able to keep Eugene out of jail for a few months by giving him another name and sending him to some sort of workfarm upstate. Their pastor, Father Rostow, had arranged it—he had Diocesan connections, and it seemed he owed Nonny a favor or two. Eugene lasted a few months but then did something awful there and was sent home. After that Nonny stayed out of trying to help Eugene (not that she stayed out of trying not to help him) but first she'd tried helping. It was amazing what she could do, and did, with a name and a few (un)official papers.

"I thought you were asleep," Renie says, coming into the room, checking a stack of books on a table for the one she needs.

"The wake is probably tonight," Nora says.

"It'll go on without you. You've already had days of being out in this weather."

"The weather won't kill me," Nora laughs.

"No, the weather probably won't," Renie says distractedly.

"But what? Going home will? You don't know anything about it. I've been sicker than this." Nora straightens herself on the sofa, feeling accused of something she can't defend herself against. Where would she start? *Just because I hear voices of the dead, the unliving, the undead, whoever they are—don't think there's anything wrong with me. I'm fine. Even if time slips like a greased knife right through my fingers, even if all these thoughts feel like bullets in my brain, I'm fine.*

"I have to be careful," she says.

"About what?" Renie asks, looking through some papers.

"About what I do or what I say, just about things."

"Listen, Nora, the strange thing is, it doesn't really help to be so careful or guarded about what you say if what you're trying to do is find missing parts of a puzzle. You can only find the pieces by spilling them all out at once and looking at what you have. You can't spill them out in careful order."

Nora hates how clever Renie is about this, how Renie won't let her just talk and comfort herself with whatever she wants to say. Nora doesn't say so, but she feels as if all the real and unreal voices, shadows, gods, charms, cures, sins, secrets are here with her now. All the dead and undead, real and unreal. "I'm just tired of not knowing—" Nora wants to stop; she knows that every word she says is dangerous and yet she tells Renie, "I'm tired of not knowing what happened."

"When?"

Nora laughs. "Well, I don't know that either." She smiles, so angry she wants to walk out of the room. She is afraid of these questions. The lessons about silence have been very strong.

"Your mother called you the night you ran from your apartment. What happened?" Papers and books on her chair, Renie is standing with her elbows resting on its winged back as she leans over the top. She is beautiful. Nora doesn't always thinks this, but there are times when she does because there is a sort of intensity that is beautiful when you see it, undiminished. And so Renie is beautiful now. And her sound is calm and confident as Nora is drawn to it though she still does not want to answer these questions. "Tell me what happened."

The directness is unbearable and Nora looks at Renie with as much rage as she can risk showing. But she admits, "This scares me."

"I know."

And then just as Nora gives in to Renie, to the questions, memory, sensing her surrender, takes Nora into itself as it has been waiting to do for years. And Nora, lying on the sofa in Renie's warm house, and warm within her fever, watches herself walk home from school, from the bus late at night, hoping no one will ever suspect the betrayal she carries with her every minute. (Not just of Eugene but of her mother, of Tessa, of herself. It is enormous and she doesn't know why.)

She opens the back door to the house, the house she grew up in. She has come home very late from school, taking the subway and two buses from Manhattan to Queens as she does every day, going to school early, coming home very late. She spends extra hours, working and reading at the university library. Every night as she comes up the driveway and in the back door into the back hall by the pantry and then into the kitchen, Nora is dead-tired. She has kept herself tired and dead for years. The 18-hour days have taken her nearly through her Ph.D. in four years, after college in three. She is a wonder. No wonder.

She's in the house for an instant, when, in the darkness, there is no movement, no sound, no one, and for a wicked second she hopes that there is no one here, that there never will be anyone here again, that she will have this place, any place and all time to herself forever. These are her secret thoughts. And she is ashamed of them, of herself even before she has locked the door and hears her father's deep voice. "Nora?" She flinches. For no reason.

"Is that you, Nora?" her father calls from the top of the stairs as Nora hangs her coat on a hook by the back door.

She doesn't answer but bends to pick up the cat. Huge, white, he falls sleepily into her arms. He is hers. Her grandfather gave him to her for her birthday the summer her mother was going to have a baby. Granhugh said the little white kitten was charmed, that he had given the cat a charm to protect Nora. He told Nora, who was five, to take care of the cat, and the cat would take care of her. Logan, the cat, named after her grandfather, *has* always taken care of Nora, as best as any charmed cat could. Logan is almost twenty years old. Like most wily cats, Logan knows how to protect himself best of all.

"Nora?" her father calls again. He never shouts. He doesn't need to. His voice has substance, layers, more layers than most people's. He has a beautiful voice really, rich for singing which he used to do when Nora and Tessa were little. Nora remembers her father waltzing her and Tessa round the room many nights when they were little. After their baths, just before bed, that was the best treat: their father holding them in turn and singing as he danced so gently that movement and music and voice were inseparable, and everything that Nora wanted, at that moment she had.

And yet now, as her father calls, she resists. "Nora?" He is impatient. Nora always waits for just that edge before she answers. "Yes," she says flatly, without inflection, without opening, merely acknowledging her own presence.

"Where were you?" her father asks, already down the stairs, sitting at the table, holding the cat, not stroking him, holding him stiffly in his lap, as if the cat is porcelain. Or as if he is dead, Nora thinks, wondering why this is happening. Logan is very still. The strange thing is that Nora is still holding the live Logan who curls into her arms as she watches her father at the table. Her father is telling her, "Your mother needs her medicine."

"Why are you so late?" her younger sister Hallie asks, suddenly appearing.

"I have to work," Nora answers.

"Work? How could you leave me here?" Hallie asks, appearing about six when she should be thirteen if Nora is twenty. "How could you?"

"I didn't know," Nora says.

"That's not true. How could you leave me?"

"I didn't know what to do."

"You didn't know to take me with you? Or to stay with me? You didn't know that?" Hallie is very upset and starting not to look like Hallie.

Nora doesn't talk. She is staring at herself.

Then memory takes Nora to the living room where she is sitting with her mother in the dark, by the window. It is the time after her mother's return (from Paris), somewhere in the ten years it took her mother to recover from her recovery, the years when her mother is dosed with medication, of all sorts, powerful stuff that overpowers her life.

Sitting in the living room by the window these nights when Nora comes home late from school, her mother will tolerate no light but whatever comes into the room from the street. And sometimes candles. A candle between them on the windowsill, Nora offers her mother her nightly cup of tea.

Nora's own cup is in her lap. Her mother looks at her, saying nothing as Nora waits like this till her mother takes the cup with both hands. Her mother asks, "Has your father eaten?" not waiting for an answer, turning away from Nora to look out the window again. In a moment, Nora watches her mother carefully bring the tea to her lips. She sips and slowly brings the cup to the saucer in her lap again. For ten years her mother has been in slow motion. But seething, with old and new fury.

Some nights she says to Nora, "Something is bothering your father. Has he said anything to you? I know he tells you and not me. He tells me nothing. But I'm glad he has you, Norie. You're a good girl." Perhaps her mother believes this. Her mother stares into the dark street. Nora has betrayed her mother: she has taken her father's confidence, though her father actually confides little, perhaps even to himself. He gets himself and his daughters through this as best he can, revealing nothing, thinking that best?

It is a brutal legacy between parent and child when things go wrong, things from the outside like illness and history that come between mother and daughter and father because that's the only place they can be healed. Is that true? It is true when you're five or ten years old, Nora thinks. And later? What happens? If the healing is slow? What's the best that comes between parent and child then? forgiveness on both sides? the child forgiving the parent for the past, the parent forgiving the child for the resentments of the present? All because we remember. Better to be cats. Porcelain cats. I don't want to remember, Nora says within the very heart of memory itself.

Remembering that she is sitting with her mother, thinking of her father who is home, upstairs, not sitting with his wife, Nora thinks that what her father loves best is laughing, and it's been hard to do that for the past few years. It would not *be*, but it would *feel* a betrayal, while his wife has been so ill. They don't talk of that, though they live with it, every day. That's the way it is. Mostly what her father asks of Nora (not because she is brighter or kinder or more generous than her sisters, which she isn't, but because Nora is the eldest and primed to be asked) are things he can't bear to do himself: medicate, watch, talk to her mother. Nora understands this; she does not resent being given these things to do, if it makes life easier for her father. She resents something but she's not quite sure what it is. She is sure however that it is the thing she resents which feels like a huge dead weight inside her. Sometimes Nora wonders if her mother is angry that Nora seems to be trusted by her father, with her father's confidences. Nora is betraying her mother for much too little. She hates herself, not her father, for that.

Her mother waits a moment as if about to say something more, but then doesn't.

Nora is aware of all the time she spends doing nothing till her mother speaks. She is aware that she is not doing nothing, that she is sitting with her mother in silence as well as sound. But it is always the silence that accuses her.

Her mother asks, "It's been dark a while. Where have you been?"

"At school."

"At school," her mother repeats, trying to fix something of the words themselves, the shape and sound, in her thought. "Yes, school." She looks out the window, drinks her tea, waits, then begins to tell Nora, "I keep thinking that my sister Peggy is getting married. In only a few days. Is that right?"

"No," Nora says softly.

"No," her mother repeats, trying to anchor herself somehow. Nora can follow much of this; it's much the same circles over and over. Watching the candle or looking out the window, but not looking at Nora, her mother says, "Well, Peggy is seeing this nice young man. Gil Delaney. He's from Ireland. But he has no family left there now. He's only twenty years old and both his parents are dead. Years ago. When Gil was just a little boy, his father dropped dead plowing his field one morning, and then months later his mother hanged herself in their kitchen. Gil found her. He had to walk to town to tell anyone. Twelve miles. He was nine years old. So awful, poor boy. He lived with an uncle after that but the uncle's dead too I think. He had no brothers or sisters. It's awful to be that alone."

Nora doesn't answer.

"You know, Norie, I don't think your grandfather likes Gil."

"They used to fight," Nora says, remembering those awful fights when her grandfather, the smaller man, would punch Gil Delaney into the kitchen wall and Gil would be stunned but not stopped, even for a moment—that's how Nora remembers it: Gil, over six feet and thick, being run into the wall by quick, wiry Granhugh who used himself as a cannon ball to hit Gil who, outraged, in the next second came at Granhugh, getting him and smashing his head with his fist. Nora, her sisters and cousins would see this on Sunday evenings, after dinner, after Mass in the morning and a day and night of men drinking whiskey. None of this is ever mentioned except when Mary Cavanaugh thinks she is in that time again.

Mary says now, as if her sister Peg were dating Gil who is already dead, "No, I don't think your grandfather likes this young man of Peg's. But he is nice, very polite, and he comes in the house. He doesn't always have to be going out somewhere, like your father. When your father comes to call on me, Norie, we leave right away. He won't stay for a cup of tea. He wants to be out. Where is your father now, Norie?"

"Upstairs."

"People keep slipping in and out of the picture. You know what I mean, Norie?"

"Yes. Maybe you're thinking of Hallie's friend, Greg," Nora says. "He came to the house the other night. He's very nice—quiet and shy but friendly. Maybe you're thinking of him."

"And Peg?"

"No, Hallie," Nora tells her mother. "Greg is Hallie's friend."

"Who is he?"

"Greg DeVito."

"What kind of name is that?"

"Italian. His father is Italian," Nora explains, realizing again how isolated they are.

"I guess that's a good thing," Mary says.

"What is?" Nora asks.

"People not crawling in on themselves, staying only with their own kind. That's what your grandmother says to do. That's what she made Peg and me do when we were getting ready to marry."

"Made you do?"

"Well, I loved your father anyway. So, it was okay. I didn't have to choose. I had my share of awful choices—but thank God that wasn't one: your father or my mother. It was okay to love your father, you see, because he was born in Ireland, you know. Your grandmother was pleased with that. She's not too pleased with your father these days though," Mary laughs. It is unexpected and gives Nora an undefined hope. "Your father never trusted your grandmother but it took her a while to see that because she was so busy being satisfied he was Irish," her mother confides. "Foolish. We shouldn't have paid attention to that, Peg and I. But it's hard to go against your mother, Norie. Even if you finally do, it's hard. And poor Peg couldn't. She couldn't go against Nonny, though she wanted to. I know she wanted to. But poor Peg. She loved this man—Milo, I think his name was. I don't remember what kind of name that was. He was born here, so I guess he was American, but his family was Greek or something—very nice people and he was a wonderful man, Norie, very good to Peggy. She loved him very much. They kept company for a long time, a couple of years, though your grandmother had no use for Milo. I think that was his name. He tried to get your grandmother to like him. He didn't see that there wasn't anything in the world he could do. He even used to bring gifts for Nonny. At first he brought all kinds of delicious pastries, Greek things, but your grandmother wouldn't eat that of course. She says rich food poisons the system. Peg and I weren't supposed to eat them either but we did, such delicious things, raspberry and chocolate rolled in pastry. Milo stopped bringing them after a while and brought flowers for your grandmother. What could you have against flowers? Milo tried very hard. And there was your father not trying at all. Your father brought nothing for your grandmother or me. Your father barely came in the door. He said he didn't come all the way from Brooklyn to be handing out gifts or drinking tea. He wanted to go to the movies or a drive or something. If I wanted to do that, then come along, he said, and I did. Picnics, your father liked picnics—"

Nora likes it when her mother has easy-flowing memories. "Picnics?" Nora asks, trying to encourage the easy sound, though by now she knows there's no determining Mary Cavanaugh's course for her.

"Picnics. Alley Pond Park, Cunningham Park. Your father liked the green grass and trees, a blanket, a few sandwiches, beer. That was the best time, Norie, the very best time. Your father had no use for sitting in the house with oldfolks—that's what he used to say. My mother must've been all of forty then," Mary laughed. Nora loves the sound. She aches for her mother. It is immediate, spontaneous, difficult.

"But I'm talking about Milo. Do you remember him? He was a handsome man. He had a large mustache—usually such an ugly thing, but not on him. He was like a character you imagine, like an actor. You know what I mean? He had a presence, I guess. Do you remember? Peggy cried for weeks when my mother wouldn't hear of their marriage. She told Peg to leave and never come back if she was going to have that man's babies. It was cruel, a cruel thing to do because Peggy loved him. And Milo's family wasn't happy about Peg either, but he would've stood up to them. And they would've been happy together, Norie, I think. It would have been better for Peg to do what she wanted. It's terrible to be so afraid, isn't it Norie? At least Peg knew what she was afraid of. She was afraid your grandmother would be angry at her and not love her, I guess. I don't know what I'm afraid of, Norie. The same thing, maybe. I think Peg still regrets Milo. She must—with all that's happened. But how could she say that? And who would want her to? But she should have been different with her girls. She should have given them a better chance than she and I had, you see. Right? But she didn't do that with Sheila. Do you remember, Norie? Remember how Peg did the same thing to Sheila when Sheila wanted to marry Nick? She ranted for weeks because Nick wasn't Irish. Where does Peggy think she and I were born? Maybe that's why we were never good enough for your grandmother either."

"Good enough?"

"From the day we were born."

"Because of where you were born?"

"Because we were born at all. I don't know. Don't ask me about this."

"It's all right."

"Peggy threatened Sheila. Remember that, how Peg threatened Sheila? You didn't know about Peg giving up Milo, did you?"

"No."

"How can people never learn? I always wondered, you know, if I could have just walked away from your father like that. I don't think so. But it was okay—he was born in Ireland, you see. Sheila was very brave wasn't she, Norie, to tell them all to go to hell, that she was marrying Nick and having whatever babies she wanted, and they better behave or they'd never see babies or her again. That was pretty smart, huh? But Peggy was too afraid to do that. After Milo, she went out and found Gil. He was born in Ireland. Sometimes I think Peggy was determined to find the worst Irishman she could—with the drinking and fighting, you know. She didn't have to. There were other good men. But maybe she thought that would make your grandmother see how good Milo was. Even before they were married Peggy and your grandmother knew about Gil Delaney's temper. They knew. But your grandmother said Gilbert Delaney was just fine. And so that's who Peggy married. Only weeks after she met him—because there was going to be a baby, you see, not Gil's baby. They always said Kath and Sheila were twins but that was the story for the priests. Kath wasn't baptised till Sheila was born. Kath was so small they could have been twins. Did you know that?"

"No."

"Peggy called today about the wedding," Mary says finally looking at Nora. "Peggy is getting married."

"Mom, Peg was married to Gil years ago before Arthur. Gil is dead and Arthur's gone. Maybe dead too, by now."

"What?"

Her mother is right: this is confusing enough without Nora adding to it. "Nothing. Gil and Arthur are both gone. That's all."

"What's that got to do with anything?" her mother asks, and Nora wonders herself what it has to do with anything at all. She also realizes that Peg probably has called today about something and that's what has set her mother thinking about all this. Peg doesn't call much these days, so it throws her mother into a spin—of time and mind— when Peg does, throws her into some part of the past when she and her sister talk all the time. Nora knows that when her mother confuses (and fuses) time and place and people there is usually a connection, a similarity, a juxtaposition of some sort in whatever time and thought her mother has mixed. It is amazing really the sense of it, of what her mother's mind does. "What did Peg call about?"

"We have to go there. Eugene has died."

"What?"

Staring out the window, her mother says again, "Eugene died this morning. I don't know anything else. Don't ask me anything else."

Nora is stunned.

"Don't ask me what happened, Norie. Don't ask me."

"I'm not asking you." But Nora asks, "When did Peg call? That's what she told you, about Eugene?"

"Eugene's dead. That's all Peggy said. That's all I know."

"What does Peg know?"

"Oh, Norie," her mother says, the effort of not crying in her voice. "Peggy would never tell me what she knows."

"Was Dad here when Peggy called? Did she talk to him?"

"No. Your father wasn't here. I was by myself. I told Peg not to tell me anything. I was by myself. I told her that. She asked if you were here, or your father, and I said no, and she said she had to tell me something, something bad, and I told her not to, Norie. I'm sorry I let her say it. Is that why it happened? Is that why this happened to Eugene?"

"No, you didn't do anything."

"Your father doesn't know. Don't tell him."

Nora is furious at her aunt for doing this to her mother. And the fury is spreading like fire crawling to the ground, spreading down and flat, about to explode. How could her aunt and grandmother have injured her mother like this without a care? "Didn't they know how dangerous it was to tell you something like this over the phone when you were by yourself?"

"Don't ask me, Nora. Don't ask me."

Nora is quiet but trembling. And then she realizes that she is more angry about the phone call than that Eugene is dead. Now she is angry at herself.

"Don't ask me, Norie," her mother says again. And Nora thinks that she doesn't know what to ask her mother if she wanted to. And she doesn't want to.

Her mother moves near. Nora moves back. They are sitting on the windowseat in the living room. The candle is burning and dripping clumps of wax down itself. Her mother sits quietly lost in the flickering light, in her myriad medicated moods, looking so small in one of the long faded nightgowns she always wears. She has been beautiful. Nora remembers that. She remembers how her mother used to hold her head back, her soft red hair waved and falling to her shoulders as she smiled and laughed. Unlike her father, whose emotion is often controlled, dampened, in her mother there was a beauty in the unrestrained joy or the comfort or wonder of the moment, and you could hear it in her voice. (And you could hear the anger, the unrestrained rage too, Nora thinks, for a split second.) *Whatever beautiful thing you find, Norie, hold onto, keep somewhere in yourself.* That's what her mother used to tell Nora, kneeling with her by the window, her mother's arms around Nora as she showed her a sunset, showing her how to look at the colors, how to feel their beauty. How to mix the colors for herself. That's who her mother was when Nora was very little. *Hold onto that,* Nora hears her say.

Her mother has put her cup and saucer on the windowsill and is folding and unfolding her hands in her lap. "He never had a chance," she says as Nora unlocks the top drawer of the big mahogany dresser that stands against the far wall of the dim living room. "Did he?" Mary Cavanaugh asks, putting her hands through her faded hair. She is worn, tired.

"No," Nora says, thinking how much she loves her mother, how much she wants her back. Nora spills out the two yellow capsules which her mother always takes at night. (Nora keeps the other pills, the ones for the morning, upstairs in her room and a few in the pocket of her own bathrobe.) She holds the ones she needs now in the palm of her hand. "Take these with a sip of tea," she tells her mother. She could give her mother fifty and she would take them. Why did Nora think such a thing? How could she? How many has she given her? One by one, her mother swallows, and then takes more, and then more, as Nora stands there and watches, and knows she should stop her, save her. But she doesn't. She is deadtired.

And then as if she hasn't been through enough, as if she doesn't need a few hours of undisturbed sleep, memory takes Nora to her sister Tessa.

In all Nora's memories there is no picture of Tessa. Tessa is a sound, a voice. A threat inside Nora. Nora feels this as she and her mother go into the kitchen and see Tessa sitting at the kitchen table, flipping the pages of a newspaper. She doesn't look up.

Nora tells her mother to sit at the table as she goes to the stove to heat the soup, slice the bread, cut some meat. Their mother doesn't sit. She is still standing by the table, looking across at Tessa, then to the window behind Tessa, then to Nora. "I shouldn't eat. I ate too much today," their mother says.

"You've eaten nothing," Tessa tells her quickly. Tessa is the rebellious one, the middle girl. For long periods of time, starting when she was about fourteen, Tessa left home to go out into parts of the world about which they had all been warned. Nora knows a few of the dangers her sister has faced by the stories Tessa has told their youngest sister Hallie. There's been days and nights lived on the streets of cities the rest of them have never been in; there's been encounters with police and threats of jail. This is only the surface and more than Nora wants to know. Always after a few weeks, there's the call to Hallie who tells Nora where to send the money. For Tessa to come home. To her room. Not to talk. For weeks. Till she leaves again. Their parents are never told anything. Tessa seldom talks to them at all. Nora never tells her parents much because Nora never mentions trouble. And Hallie tells nothing because she is only thirteen and mostly talked to, though it's Hallie who knows most of Tessa's secrets. "I've been here all day," Tessa says. "You've eaten nothing."

"Just ignore it, Tess, please—" Nora says, as if Tessa can ignore the rage she feels at them all, especially Nora for telling her to be good, as if that will protect them.

Tessa laughs.

Nora turns from the stove. "What is it?"

But Tessa doesn't look up. "And another thing," Tessa says, flipping a page, "she never sits still." Tessa talks about their mother as if she's not there. "Just watch her, rocking back and forth like a damn swing. What's the matter with her? Can anyone tell me that?"

"It's hard enough," says Nora, not looking at either of them. "Just ignore it." Nora's not sure if she's talking to Tessa, her mother, herself. She's not sure who she should protect here, knowing she's protecting no one.

When her father comes down the stairs into the kitchen, Tessa leaves, her mother finally sitting at the table in this same endless night— all those nights. Her father is sullen, though still handsome, with an angular face and deepset green eyes. Nora detects a shadowy strength buried in his doubts about them and himself. She wishes he wouldn't doubt, wishes he would trust something though she wouldn't know what to tell him to trust in.

"You shouldn't be late," he tells her. "It upsets your mother."

Nora avoids his eyes. She can do nothing. She feels herself tumble backward down a hillside while her father watches. Helpless. Till she stops falling.

Edward Cavanaugh doesn't see that his attempt to avoid all dangers, all dark tunnels, takes him just as long and keeps him watching nothing but the ground.

Nora remembers seeing her father sitting alone in his room upstairs. Many nights he's in his chair, playing his old Irish records, usually some John McCormick ballad, reading his Irish newspapers that his brothers in Ireland send him. Edward Cavanaugh has nine brothers, none in this country. Some nights her father opens his whiskey cabinet. But usually not. Usually he just sits with his music and his papers. Nora remembers seeing him in there one night when she was coming upstairs to go to bed. He didn't seem to notice how dark the room was getting. His head was back, his eyes closed, a drink forgotten in his hand. If she had gone in, touched his hand, asked him what was going to happen, he would've pulled back, not out of the despair but from disclosing it as if it were shameful, and not something they shared.

*

Nora gets up slowly from the sofa, going to the fire, to the mantelpiece.

"What are you doing?" Renie asks.

Nora holds the ledge, staring at the white wood and marble, wondering if her grandfather has made this mantel. Her grandfather made such beautiful furniture. She used to watch him. He was a careful carpenter—like St. Joseph. "Whatever happened to St. Joseph after Jesus died? You never hear anything. Whole family die out?" These are questions Granhugh asks about St. Joseph, and Nora realizes only now how much they must have bothered him because he always got around to asking them of any priest he met. She is so smart; she's read so many books, seen so many connections, allusions, echoes—and for thirty years she's missed that her grandfather (a good and careful carpenter) has wanted to know about St. Joseph, that good, careful man, who took on being the father (though he wasn't the father) to the child Jesus. *What happens to him?* her grandfather asks. "Doesn't that count? being someone's father for thirty years? someone's grandfather? Doesn't that get you a story?"

Well, it depends on who's saving the stories, Nora thinks, realizing that her grandfather has always known this, has known that everyone's got stories but not all are saved. Being saved depends on many things, but not usually the beauty or truth of your story, or we'd still be telling stories of goddesses. Mostly being saved depends on how you and your story fit in with all the rest that's being saved, how your voice blends, not soars. But she doesn't have to tell her grandfather this. He knows that all the stories and lives that led to his own will be lost unless he saves them. He knows that for all the reality, presence, influence his stories are meant to have in this family, he might as well be as dead as these stories will be unless he tells them, tells someone who will tell about him. He has been telling Nora.

"Nora—" Renie is standing by Nora at the fireplace.

"I'm okay." She crosses her arms on the mantel and puts her head down. This was all beginning to pull together somehow. All the stories—Granhugh's, Nonny's, her own—were threads of the same circle. If she follows the clearest line, it will take her round the others to the center, that deep hole of secrets Nora has been avoiding for years. But she can't live on the rim anymore. She is going to fall one way or the other, out of, or into this real and unreal world she's been born to.

Nora reaches for one of the silver picture frames on the mantel and holds it. She doesn't want it to fall. If she's not careful there will be shards of glass all over the floor.

"Nora, let go," Renie says, putting her hands over Nora's. "It's going to break, Nora—" Slowly Nora takes her hands from the picture, unable to stop trembling.

"Lie down," Renie says, walking Nora back to the sofa.

There is a sort of urgency in Nora as Renie puts the blanket over her, saying or asking Nora something as if sleep isn't the only call Nora can answer right now. "I need to sleep. My mother has her medicine, everyone is safe, I can sleep."

For a while. But not for long. "Norie?"

Nora looks up. Her mother is standing by the bed. "Norie?"

Nora gets out of bed, looking at the clock: 3:15. At least she's not crying. Nora pulls on her robe. The room is chilly. Nora hates getting up on cold nights. But she knew this would happen, with Tessa upsetting her mother like that.

"Norie?"

"Yes, it's okay," Nora says, as she takes her mother out of the room. Nora knows her mother won't go back to her own bed. They go downstairs to the kitchen.

"I don't know why this always happens," her mother says, sitting at the table, twisting her hair for a moment, saying nothing until, "I don't understand. I wake up so scared."

"Did you have a nightmare?"

"I don't know. I just get so scared. What's going to happen, Norie?"

Nora takes the little plastic bottle of pills from the pocket of her robe where she keeps them, and gives her mother one. Just one extra, Nora thinks. "Here."

"Did you sleep at all?" Nora asks seriously, needing to know, to gauge the pattern of nights and days, to anticipate change. A night and then another without sleep brings the bottom of the cycle. This is even more dangerous than what Nora thinks of as the top of the cycle—the days when her mother moves frantically around the house turning on all the lights, saying she needs more light, "More light!" to stop the darkness. When those days come Nora is always grateful her mother is too afraid to leave the house. "Imagine having to look for her around the neighborhood?" she usually asks Hallie, who would be the one to help her.

"Yes, I slept," her mother tells Nora seriously—she knows the point. She knows too that it's the sleepless nights that signal the terrified state when she's likely to want to hurt herself. It's good that she's able to wake Nora when this happens. It's good that it helps that Nora sits with her. Even her mother says this. When Nora decided to take the teaching job three hundred miles away, everyone (in the world, in her world) thought it would kill her mother. No one, especially her mother, knew how Mary Cavanaugh would manage. But within a few months her mother had more than managed: she'd awakened. Well, she had already secretly started to wean herself off these godawful pills. (The pills Nora will have to give her more of now, even knowing that her mother is doing better without them years later? Time is mingled, as if there is no time.) This night, so many nights later, Nora sits with her mother in the kitchen at 3:00 a.m. asking the quieting questions she learned to ask. "Do you want some milk or tea?" The kitchen is cold in the early dark morning.

"Will you be late today?" her mother asks, folding and unfolding her hands but they still shake. "Maybe you don't have to go today." When she was six or seven, just before and after Hallie was born, her mother used to keep Nora home from school for weeks at a time, afraid to let her go to school she always said, but maybe her mother was afraid to be alone, or to be home by herself with the baby. Maybe she kept Nora home because no one else came to help her with the crying she couldn't bear to hear. Mary Cavanaugh saved Hallie by keeping Nora home from school. In the midst of the craziness, her mother tried to protect them, from herself.

"I won't be too late," Nora tells her mother.

"Can you call Peggy? Ask her or your grandmother to come today?"

"I don't know," Nora says, knowing she will not call her aunt or grandmother. She has learned not to ask for what will not be given.

"We have to go to the wake. We have to go there today. Don't you know that?" But her mother isn't upset. She says this calmly because it is a mistake. This hasn't happened yet. It has to be a mistake. How can Eugene be dead? It's a mistake. Nora is sure. She knows it is all a mistake. And even her mother knows this as she says, "You know we have to go to the wake today. Are you afraid?"

Why would her mother ask her that? But then Nora knows it is a mistake, *and* true, and it is her fault. No one understands this yet, but Nora knows it now in a split second of certainty which is gone as swiftly as it has come— swiftly simply in a strangely exquisite stroke: the mind itself understanding; the mind understanding itself.

"Nora, the light hurts." *Light, at night, through the trees. Light, like ice, like glass through the trees. Don't go. Don't move.*

Nora turns off the overhead fluorescent kitchen lights and switches on the small counter light by the sink. Nearly in the dark, her mother begins to speak, the voice circling Nora in the dimness, haunting her.

"Don't leave me here," she yells. Like Eugene.

Nora woke up screaming. She dreamt she was screaming and trying to wake up but couldn't. She is sitting on the couch, Renie trying to hold her as Nora fights. Renie is shaking Nora by the shoulders, saying her name. Hearing her name, Nora pulls herself toward it, pulling herself awake. She is sore and scared. She hasn't dreamt that.

"It's okay," Nora says, trying to sound as if she means this, but not as she means everything now, desperately, as if her life depends on it.

If Nora had a candle, she'd light it.

IV. *Disintegration, Cures And Why the Banshee Wails*

𝕳𝖔𝖑𝖉𝖎𝖓𝖌 the soup bowl to her chin, Nora sips slowly before biting into a carrot and then a piece of potato flavored with pepper and garlic. The taste is tremendous, the pleasure reassuring as she eats. She is relaxed as she tells Renie, "I remember a few months after Eugene's wake—"

Legs folded on her chair, soup bowl in her hand, Renie stops eating. Her sharp green eyes stay on Nora. "When did Eugene die?"

"About six years ago."

"Six years ago?" Renie stares.

"I think. It's hard to say. We never mention it."

"Six years?"

"It feels like yesterday. I've heard people say that: it feels like yesterday—and who believes it or knows how true it is? After six years, it hits me that *Eugene is dead. Dead?* That it's not a mistake, or it doesn't matter if it is—he's not coming back no matter how much you talk about the dead coming back, no matter how many stories you tell about shadowgods or holy charms curing the incurable, Eugene's not coming back."

"You thought he would come back?"

"Well, I guess I thought it was all a mistake and it would get fixed."

"What was a mistake?"

"That Eugene got into that fight, that he got himself killed." But as soon as Nora says this she knows it's part of the official story, the one they've all been telling for six years. It has little to do with what happened, whatever that was.

She knows it as clearly as she knows that she stood near her aunt, Eugene's mother, at the wake and had overheard her tell and retell the other part of the official family story: "Eugene died defending his girlfriend. From attack. By a stranger. Late at night. The man fled. Eugene got back to his room and died in the night. We found him the next morning." Without a mark on him, Nora thinks, knowing that that truth and all the questions it opened about the fight to the death Eugene was supposed to have had with a stranger over the life of his girlfriend—whom none of them knew—was never part of the official family story. Nora has heard this story so often it is the one that immediately comes to mind; it is the story that makes her wonder if by now the story has grown to include the honor not only of all womanhood but of his country too: did Eugene die defending his country, flying the most dangerous mission over enemy territory at night, the single fighter, the single volunteer fighter out of how many men? That's what Eugene's story has been about, from the time he was born: being a man. The only son, the only grandson. The savior, of them all, from sins, fate, the inevitability they ensured?

Eugene's father, Gil Delaney, was harsh on all his children. "Don't baby the boy," Gil would say when Eugene was only a baby and wanting his mother. "Don't baby him or he'll be useless. Give him a crack for that yelling so he'll know what to cry for." And when Eugene was a bit older, three or so, Gil would whack him if Eugene weren't being as tough as Gil thought he should be. The only child of a poor Irish farmer, Gil's own father had died in the fields and his mother hanged herself in their kitchen before Gil was nine.

Renie is waiting for Nora to explain something about Eugene when Nora remembers: *The coroner reported suspicious substances, not the usual drugs, not heroin or cocaine or whatever kids were taking six years ago to kill themselves. It was something very odd, hard to trace, hard to prove. Something ancient? Something police and even pathologists weren't looking for and didn't find except for the suspicion.*

She admits now, "Eugene was found dead, or dying. It's hard to know. My grandmother was there that morning. That always complicates things. If you're trying to get to the center of something and you run into my grandmother, you've got a tangled trip ahead of you."

"You think it was a mistake but it might not have been an accident?"

Nora waits for the words she's secretly held for years to stop echoing inside her. "Yes."

"And you think your grandmother might be behind the not-accident?"

"You're beginning to see how things are—or how they're said, or not-said in this family, anyway," Nora laughs, wondering how any of this could be funny. "Kathleen knew there was something strange about the morning Eugene died. Her room was next to her brother's, and that morning she heard her mother in the hall talking to Nonny. It was very early. Peg sounded upset and Kathleen went to see what was going on. The door to Eugene's bedroom was open and Nonny was in the room sitting on the bed. 'What's going on?' Kath whispered, catching a glimpse of her brother's face: *Eugene was laughing and then something happened and Eugene's head went back with a laugh that seemed to stitch his side the way some laughs do, and Eugene put his hand to the place where the laugh caught him because by now, a second later, there was some awful pain and contortion in his face, and he was so surprised to know that he was about to die, because he must have realized that with that kind of pain it could happen and then did. In a second. The way huge irrevocable things do. In a second. He was just so surprised and then not surprised at all. Then he said, 'Oh, I knew it,' as if pleased with himself.*

"Kathleen said it was quiet then, her brother seemed to be sleeping and Nonny was sitting very calmly watching him when suddenly Nonny told Kathleen to call the police. Kath thought Nonny must have said to call the doctor. But Nonny said, 'No, not the doctor, the police. Go. Do what you're told.' Kath said she couldn't understand any of it. She just wanted to understand one thing that was happening because maybe then it wouldn't seem so awful. But she couldn't understand anything. For a moment she thought Nonny was going to have her brother arrested. She said that she really thought her mother and grandmother were trying to get the police there to take Eugene away before he woke up.

"Kathleen wanted to warn him and was about to reach for him when my grandmother told her again: 'Move— call the police.' And when Kathleen didn't, my grandmother, angry and forgetting herself for the first time in her life, stood up, a half-empty bottle of whiskey falling to the floor. Kath reached for it, at that moment realizing her brother was dead. Kathleen said she finally had something to understand. 'What have you done?' she asked my grandmother who, composed again, told Kathleen to watch herself and what questions she asked."

"You think the whiskey killed your cousin?"

"No. I think something in the whiskey killed him."

"Didn't the police check the whiskey for poison?"

"They never knew about the bottle."

"Kathleen didn't tell the police?"

"Tell them what my grandmother didn't want told? Her brother was dead. Maybe from telling what my grandmother didn't want told."

Renie leans forward in her chair as if bringing the present to Nora, or Nora back to some point in the present. "Your mother didn't call you about Eugene the other night, did she?"

"No." Nora closes her eyes. Her head is pounding. "But maybe Eugene will come back and straighten this out. Maybe he'll explain this to Hallie at least. He was closest to Hallie. They were babies together. He never turned on her, never threatened her—"

"Who did he threaten?"

"Oh, himself mostly. But I don't know. I didn't live in my grandmother's house. I didn't know about all the trouble. It seems there was always trouble.

"I remember Hallie telling me that she and Eugene were about nine or ten when they were playing with a group of kids on the roof of an apartment house one summer. They found a couple of cats up there one day and the kids started teasing the cats and then it got worse and they wanted to throw the cats off the building—to see what would happen. Hallie started pleading with them not to but they started to dangle one of the cats over the edge of the roof. Eugene told them to stop, but they laughed at him. Hallie said he got up, without a word, and took the cat away from the kid who had it. And then all of a sudden, before anyone knew what was happening, he took the kid by the feet and dangled him from the roof. They were twenty storeys up. No one, even Hallie, was sure Eugene wouldn't drop the kid. He didn't, but Eugene held the boy there quite a long time. He made the kid meow.

"By the time he was twelve he was out of any kind of control. He hit his stepfather Arthur to the floor once in one blow."

"Who?"

"Haven't I mentioned Arthur?"

"No, never."

"Oh, well we didn't know him very long. Peg married him a few years after Gil died. Arthur was gone by the time my cousin Sheila got married, so he didn't stay long. We were too strange for him, I guess, though Arthur was pretty strange himself. He sold fish. Tropical fish, pets. He tried to train them. He started putting fish tanks—huge things, all over my grandmother's house. Peg and Arthur lived at Nonny's of course. Well, one day Granhugh couldn't take any more fish. He said they smelled, and they couldn't be trained worth a damn and what kind of a thing was that for a man to be doing? By the fifteenth or sixteenth tank, he said Arthur was insane and someone had to do something. My grandfather did—he came home with a truck one afternoon while Arthur was at work, loaded the tanks on the truck, and we never saw a fish in the house again after that. Arthur left a few weeks later I think. He was nice—very polite, didn't drink much, but he and Peg used to fight quite a lot anyway. Not screaming and hitting like Peg and Gil, but fighting. Anyway, Eugene couldn't stand Arthur, though I don't think Arthur ever did anything to him. Arthur certainly never beat him the way his father used to. But Eugene wasn't taking any chances—Eugene started hitting first, to let Arthur know who would be doing the hitting I guess if it was going to be done. Maybe something did happen between them, but I never heard about it. But I saw Eugene hit Arthur to the floor once. Eugene wasn't even thirteen then but he was already six feet. Arthur was stunned. He didn't go after Eugene; he didn't try to knock him down. He probably knew he'd be killed. Come to think of it, maybe that's why he left, not because of the fish."

Nora remembers seeing Eugene fight someone, probably Arthur, in the snow early one morning in her grandmother's backyard. Eugene hit the man into the snow and then hit him again when the man tried to get up, ferociously pounding him, and then standing over him when the man was unable to move and lay bleeding. *Move and I'll make it hurt more.* Eugene wiped the back of his hand across his mouth, as if satisfied with a good job.

Or maybe it was Nora who was satisfied watching Eugene doing the pounding because there was another time too, an early summer morning when Nora, going up her grandmother's driveway, saw Eugene and the same man fighting. What disturbed Nora that day was not the battle, which she left without a word, letting Eugene pound the man, whoever he was, Nora glad to see it happening even as she knew it couldn't really be happening which is the thing that disturbed her: she wanted to see this beating so much she was imagining it, which is what she might have thought except that three days later Eugene was dead.

And it all seemed Nora's fault which she doesn't say now as she eats more soup and talks to Renie, keeping secret how she saw her cousin fighting and told no one. "Hallie was the only one who could talk to Eugene. She wasn't afraid of him. If you were afraid of him, Eugene ate you up. I guess that was his way of not being afraid. Hallie told me once about waking up one night terrified that someone was in her bedroom. She said she woke out of a sleep with the feeling that someone was staring at her. She was afraid to open her eyes, and when she did she saw someone: a man standing at the foot of her bed. It took a second to realize that it was okay, that it was Eugene, and another second to remember that he was dead. He stayed only a minute, and said nothing. She said she had the feeling he'd been watching her for a while before she woke up. He came back the next night—and she wasn't afraid. She asked him what he wanted. That was the feeling she had looking at him, that he wanted to tell her something, and wanted something from her. He kept looking at her, and then he started to move towards her, looking as if he were standing still, but coming near. This scared her, and he looked hurt by that and faded away, without saying anything. He came back about a year later, but he didn't say anything then either. He just wanted to see her I guess.

"People don't always stay dead," Nora says, her steadiness slipping. "I remember the night my mother went to Paris—"

"Paris?"

"That's all my sisters and I were ever told. 'Your mother needs a rest,' my grandmother told us. 'Do you remember how your mother liked to paint? Well, painters go to Paris.' I guess she just said it on the spur of the moment. She couldn't have planned to tell us such a thing. And we were so confused by everything I guess Paris seemed reasonable and it's just always been the way I've thought of my mother being away. Hallie does too, now that I think of it. She probably picked it up from me. But if we mention that time at all, we say, 'Oh, that was when Mom was in Paris.' My mother's fine now. She had a long struggle, but she's okay. She doesn't seem to remember this at all."

"You want her to?"

"No," Nora says immediately.

"It would be understandable if you wanted your mother to remember, don't you think?"

"None of this is understandable. It was a nightmare. I don't wish it on her." And then Nora asks about Renie's daughter because again she has an awful urge to hurt Renie. "Do you think the pain Emma inflicts on you is understandable?"

"I suppose Emma understands it."

"That's not what I asked."

"I know what you're asking," Renie says, sounding tired. "Emma probably wants to hurt me. Is that what you want me to say?"

"I'm sorry." And she is.

All these thoughts are tangled in memories of her mother's leaving, and Nora's enormous resistance to the memory, but Nora can't even explain that now because no matter how she tries not to, she is seeing the doctor come into Nonny's house the night her mother left.

She has never told anyone of this: the doctor, an old, stooped man with lots of gray hair, standing in their grandmother's kitchen, Nora's father sitting at the table, defeated, as her mother walks furiously, ferociously round the room, talking and talking and then yelling.

"The doctor was getting an injection ready," Nora says, putting her nearly finished bowl of soup on the table. "That's how they finally got my mother to be quiet. My grandfather wanted to give her whiskey, and the doctor got even angrier with them all."

Pieces keep beginning, against each other, Nora remembering details she's taken in without knowing it. All of a sudden, after twenty years, it is all here: "My Aunt Peg managed to get my sisters and cousins upstairs but my mother was too near me. I was beneath the table in the kitchen, hiding. My father and grandfather were afraid to reach for me, to make any sudden movement. She was screaming and no one knew what to do. When she picked up a knife, my grandmother called the doctor, my mother screaming the whole time. Even when the doctor came, they couldn't make my mother stop yelling."

Nora wonders if she seems crazy to Renie; she is trying to sound very controlled, very clear, deliberately slowing her pace, keeping her hands tightly folded under the blanket. "My father got the knife away from my mother, and the doctor gave her an injection, and then my grandmother thanked him and said he could leave. But the doctor was going nowhere without my mother. He asked why they had waited so long, how they could have left my mother alone in a house with three children. Hallie was about four, Renie. My mother had been getting like this for more than four years. The doctor knew. He told them, 'No one gets like this over night.' He knew. He saw everything the minute he walked in the door, and he told them, 'No one, not overnight,' filling the syringe again. My grandmother was answering no questions. After the doctor gave my mother the second injection, my grandmother started explaining that my mother was just overtired and confused but that she was fine. That's what she said. My mother was afraid of her own shadow, her own voice, she thought people wanted to kill her, she talked to God day after day, she thought Satan was living with us, she thought he called on the phone. . . . One night she pulled the phone out of the wall and she had been getting like that for years, for *four years,* Renie, and my grandmother said she was fine. I was out from under the table, and my mother was sedated, or dead. I didn't care."

"You cared," Renie says.

"No, I really didn't. Don't give me any credit for caring what happened to her. I didn't."

"You cared," Renie says again. "You wanted her gone—"

"No—"

"You wanted the nightmare to stop."

"How do you know what I wanted?"

"You were furious—"

"Why do you keep saying I'm angry? I'm not angry!" Nora feels as if she's screamed but it is barely a shout.

"No, you sound perfectly unangry." Renie is sitting back in her chair, her legs folded against each other, her eyes on Nora.

"I remember my mother that hot summer before Hallie was born—that was the beginning, Renie. That's when it all started. I remember her sitting at the kitchen table, not a breeze coming through the curtains, the relentless sun everywhere, my mother's face already so swollen and wet with sweat it was hard to know when she was crying. 'Why doesn't anyone help me?' she'd ask Nonny or her sister Peg when they came.

"'What do you think I'm doing?' Peg would say, getting mad.

"'It looks as if you're doing the dishes,' my mother would answer as her sister stood at the sink or cleared the table. And I remember my mother, in all seriousness, asking, 'Do you think doing the dishes is going to help me? Is that what you think I need to do?'

"'You need to take care of this house, these babies, and yourself,' Peg told her. 'Look at you. When was the last time you were out of that bathrobe? What's the matter with you?'

"'My outfits don't fit,' my mother said, feeling hopeless and embarrassed. Even I could tell that, Renie. But Peg didn't give up. 'You have maternity clothes, from Tessa—' she told my mother.

"My mother laughed. 'You think I can put those clothes on, after what I went through the last time? You think I'd ever wear those clothes again? You think I'm crazy?'

"'Yes,' her sister answered.

"My mother started to laugh. 'I need a mirror,' she told Peg. 'To show you how ridiculous *you* look, standing there doing dishes for a crazy woman, while that woman is dying—'

"'No one is dying,' Peg shot back.

"'No one?' my mother asked. 'Do you remember the last time, Peggy, with Tessa? Do you remember how little she was? Three pounds and blue. Do you remember that? Well, this baby doesn't even have that chance. That's what those doctors told me. They told me no more babies. I told Father Rostow. I told him what would happen. I went to him a year ago—'

"'You what?' This made Peg angry. She finally looked at my mother who hadn't moved from the kitchen table. Peg was still at the sink but she turned to look at my mother and ask her, very seriously, 'What did you tell him? He knows all of us, you know, Mary. You were telling him about all of us. What's the matter with you? Don't you have any shame?'

"'Oh, stop worrying.' my mother told her. 'Father Rostow didn't know what I was talking about. He thought I was talking about sin. I was trying to tell him about living and dying, about having two babies already and leaving them motherless. That's the sin, Peg. But the good Father didn't see that, so now he's part of it, because something awful is going to happen here, Peg.' I remember my mother asking, 'How can it be wrong if I told him the truth?'

"Peg didn't want to hear about truth. What did truth have to do with telling people, with telling priests things that were no one's business? That's all she wanted to ask my mother. And she wanted to know what my mother had said. She wanted to know what was being said about her family. 'What truth?' Peg asked, getting even angrier. 'Why can't you just do what you're supposed to? You're supposed to take care of this house and these children. Millions of women do it, but it's too much for you. Why? Because you're special? Because you're some sort of special artist or painter or whatever you are, or thought you were? Well, you're not so special. Just because a few teachers told you they thought you had talent, you thought you were a great artist, a Picasso or somebody. Well, you're not. You're a great nothing. Everyone knew that—even that friend of yours, Lillian. Even Lillian Bead knew you were nothing special. She felt sorry for you is all. I heard her tell her other friends how sorry she felt for you.'

"'That's not true,' my mother said. 'Lillian is my friend.' But my mother was hurt. I could see that, Renie. She didn't say much as Peg kept pounding her, asking my mother: 'Why can't you just do what you're supposed to? Why can't you just behave?'

"But just when I thought my mother couldn't say another word, she looked right at her sister, her hands tapping the table as she asked, 'Why can't I be good like you, Peggy? Is that what you're asking me? Why can't I be good like you?'

"'Yes,' Peg told her, not realizing as I did that my mother was ready to strike.

"'Good like you so I can be as happy as you? Is that what you're telling me, Peg? To be good like you, do all I'm supposed to for house, husband, children and then I'll be happy like you? Well, it's not my face that has to do all the healing,' my mother said, giving Aunt Peg a chance to say nothing. I wasn't suprised my mother could hit back like that. I knew how fast she could be with words. I knew she could hurt you with words just like Peg and Nonny if she wanted. But I was still surprised by what she said. No one ever mentioned Peg's bruises. I remember my mother's hands slapping the table. 'Not my face Peggy that ever looks like that.'

"'Go to hell,' Peg said. 'Just go to hell. You think you're so superior. At least I'm not sitting in my bathrobe all day, unable to feed or dress my children.'

"'Yes, at least you're not doing that. I guess I should have told Father Rostow how well you're doing. I could call him now. Do you want me to do that, to call him on the phone and tell him that he shouldn't think there's anything wrong with you just because he thought I was crazy? Should I tell him how well Gil's doing? How he's been fired from three jobs this year but none of it was Gil's fault? How he threw you down a flight of stairs a few months ago but that's not poor Gil's fault either? Should I—'

"'You shut up. You just shut up. You don't know what you're talking about. You're really crazy, you know that?'

"'Yes'

"'Well then just shut up.'

"'I can't. I've tried. It doesn't help to just shut up. Nothing changes. A year ago I knew this would happen and I tried to tell Father Rostow but that was crazy, and now this is crazy. And it just keeps getting more crazy because no one does anything. All they tell me is, "Look for signs. Come to the hospital at the first sign," they tell me. Well, I have signs and dreams, Peggy. You know I've always had dreams. Now I dream we're all going to burn in hell for this. And it's true. I know it's true. It's already true. And you think I should pick out a nice dress and do the dishes. I need a mirror, Peggy, so I can show you how silly that is. So you can all see how crazy *you* are. And then, when I've got you all in there, I can smash it, smash the mirror into little pieces all over the floor. And then you'll all be gone, and I won't be crazy anymore. That's what I want Peg. Think sweeping the floor will help? Is that what you think?'

"'I don't know what to think of you anymore, Mary.'

"'I bet you don't.'

"'What do you want us to do?'

"'Help me.'

"'Help you what? I don't know what we're talking about. And I don't want to know. We're not that kind of people.'

"That's when my mother grabbed her good teacup and threw it at her sister. It went past Peg and hit the wall, splattering tea and cup everywhere. My mother was very calm then. 'What kind of awful people are we, Peg? What kind?'

"My mother felt herself slipping away, Renie. She was terrified of having another baby. She nearly died having Tessa who nearly died too. She went to Father Rostow for some kind of help, for permission for contraception (another sin) to save her life but the good Father didn't know anything about my mother's life. I was seven years old but I knew that, sitting in that oak panelled room listening to the lecture on sin and responsibility and God's purpose. I knew Father Rostow didn't know what it was to have a baby cry all night every night for weeks. He didnt know what it was to watch my mother cry because everything felt bad.   All he knew was sin and that's all my mother remembered, feeling it was sin she had conceived as punishment for all the sins she'd ever committed. I think that's how it got twisted, Renie. Because she was terrified. That much I know.

"'Don't leave me here, Peg,' I remember my mother saying, folding and unfolding her hands, saying she would get dressed, she would do the dishes, she would do anything. *Just don't leave me here.*

"But someone couldn't always be there. There were days and days when it was just me and my mother—"

"And Tessa?" Renie asks. "Where was Tessa?"

"Well, she must have been there too. She was just a baby, but I can't remember her." And Nora finally admits: "I must have done something so awful to her, Renie, I can't remember her."

"Done what? You were only five or six."

"It must have been awful because they had to get Tessa out of there."

"Not because of anything you were doing."

"I don't know."

"Who had to get Tessa out of there?"

Nora thinks of her grandmother coming to the house that summer. "Nonny came very early, before work. Mostly my grandmother tried to show my mother how to clean, as if my mother had forgotten and my grandmother thought that was the problem. By the end, my mother wasn't cleaning, or cooking, or even taking me to school. By the end, she didn't seem to know who she was or where we were. I don't remember much about this, but I remember that by the end, when my grandmother would leave after a few hours with us, she didn't leave alone. I don't remember Tessa because Tessa wasn't there," Nora says, with relief. She moves the blanket away as if she is going to stand, as if now she is strong enough because for the first time in twenty years, she is relieved about this. "I was always afraid I'd done something horrible to Tessa. But I didn't. I didn't do anything. She wasn't there. That's all. That's why I can't remember her."

"Your grandmother took Tessa."

"Yes. I thought I'd done something so awful to Tessa I couldn't remember her. But I didn't. She really wasn't there, that's all. I guess she usually came back at night, with my father. Tessa must have been dropped off with a neighbor or somebody who was watching her. I guess that's why my grandmother came all those mornings before work—not only to check on my mother, but to take Tessa wherever Tessa was being taken. My father left much too early in the morning to take her I guess. My grandmother had to come by a few hours later for Tessa. I suppose they thought I was going to school. But usually I wasn't, and not in the summer. I wouldn't be going to school in the summer. . . ."

"Your grandmother took your sister and left you," Renie says, pushing Nora to realize this because Renie knows that *being left* is the part Nora has avoided seeing for more than twenty years.

"Yes," Nora says, wanting to feel the relief again but it's already turned into something else, the awful past blankness filling with what she's wanted most not to feel all these years: "Yes, my grandmother left me there."

Nora is stunned. "I don't know how this started," she says, meaning these pictures, remembering that she's been talking about her mother's pictures, her mother's days of painting, but also meaning that she wants to retract what she's just pictured: her grandmother at the door, Tessa in her arms, Nora watching her leave. That's what she begins to tell Renie about again, after a moment. Not knowing how she is telling this, Nora braces herself, pulling back to an appearance of strength she does not feel and comforts herself as she speaks with the thought that the blank pieces are finding shape.

Some kind of shape. And in a way Nora doesn't understand at all, the knowing (even of abandonment) gives her an anchor in this storm of a story which is already moving to another scene. Brushing her damp hair out of her eyes, Nora tells Renie, "I remember my mother painting in the backyard, for the light. Or in dark weather, she'd be in the dining room, nothing on the dining room table but her paints and oils and sketches. Some days we'd be charcoal all over, the both of us, from her sketches. It was wonderful. It was remarkable what she could do. Magical. I remember watching and wondering how she knew so much, my mother. And then thinking: this is my mother, and she knows this magic, and I'll know it too, because she's my mother. It was a feeling of being inside something tremendous, a moment of awareness, of myself, of time, of something beyond everything. I was only about six, and of course, I didn't know that that's what any of this was, but that's what it was, whether I could explain it or not, to anyone. And there was something tremendous about her paintings. Some were like cartoons— bright reds, yellows, round people. Things jumping out at you, people and motion exaggerated, comical and threatening at the same time. And others were very real things, pictures of houses, lots of houses probably all the houses she lived in as a little girl."

Nora watches Renie ladle more soup out of the tureen that sits by the glass vase in the middle of the square oak coffee table. "Thanks," Nora says bringing the soup bowl near her mouth, then spooning it cool as the story went on, through her but on its way through circles of time and memory and events, Nora already telling Renie, "Granhugh always made the decision about moving. It was my grandfather who owned the house they lived in when they got married. My grandmother had no house. Before she met my grandfather, she and her two daughters were living in the nurses quarters of the hospital where my grandmother was studying. They were hiding. And tired of it. And my grandfather was tired of this country. His first wife had just died; the bootleg business he'd been in with my grandmother's brother Laurence was over; there was nothing here, so my grandfather was going back to Ireland. He barely knew my grandmother but her dead brother Laurence Doyle had been good to my grandfather, taking him into the bootleg and all, so Hugh Logan told my grandmother that she and her daughters could have the house. And he meant it. It wasn't his fault that the Second World War broke out the next day and he couldn't get out of the country. The steamship people were sending no ships. So, my grandfather was in a bind—he'd given away his house but he hadn't sold it. My grandfather had no money to buy or even rent another house, so, he went back to my grandmother and told her he was stuck here, which he knew wasn't her fault, but here he was, and that wasn't his fault, so if she wanted to stay in the house, maybe they should get married. He told her he'd probably be taken in the army any day and be dead in a few weeks anyway, so it wasn't going to be much of a marriage—just for the house and look of the thing for the girls. My grandmother agreed to it.

"They lived in many houses after that because it was all still in my grandfather's name. If he had no other hold over Ursula Doyle, he could sell any house they had out from under her. If she thought she controlled everything, made all the decisions and rules, he could show her. He'd come home and announce he'd sold the house. I guess that's why he always did it: because he could. And my grandmother probably kept waiting, but there was no army for Hugh Logan. And my mother started dreaming of houses and painting them. No wonder she never quite got over looking for home."

Nora remembers her grandfather saying that Mary Cavanaugh was as sad and lost as a banshee, those harmless spirits who often haunt houses and whose laments are very powerful. *The bean sidhe's never wrong. If you hear that cry, listen. It's meant to warn you,* he told her. Nora never asked why no one listened to her mother's lament, *bean sidhe* spirit or not.

"When I was very young, there was something very wrong and very wonderful about my mother. The wrong and the wonderful couldn't be separated really in her and the painful part took over for a while, but there was a time when there was something very fascinating, some sort of extraordinary attempt in my mother. That's the only way I can think of it. That's what she must have been like when my father met her. At a church dance. He wasn't even out from Ireland a year. And here was this woman—lively, energetic, funny, smart, with an unmatchable imagination and spirit. My mother must have seemed perfect, for reasons he didn't even see. He just loved her. He wanted a life with her. Their own life. He must've thought that's what they'd have. But after a while, my father saw that he and my mother would never have a life together if my mother didn't break the awful hold my grandmother had on her. He waited for this and after a while I know that he insisted on this, that my mother break the hold my grandmother had, or break with him. He said it had to be done. I remember him saying that. And he was right: my grandmother's hold had to be wrenched; she was not going to let go.

"My father tried to help my mother pull herself away, I think. And my mother tried, as hard as it was, as terrifying as it was (because my mother was afraid of her mother), my mother did try to break from my grandmother, because she loved my father. And that was the choice: husband or mother. I don't think she remembers that now. Her sister Peggy had to choose Nonny over the man she wanted to marry, a man named Milo whom Peggy gave up. The choice had been put to my mother too and my father saw that the choice was killing her, and would kill her because my grandmother's reach went deep inside my mother and my mother was tearing herself apart and tearing out parts of herself because she couldn't see where my grandmother's hold stopped and her own began. As my grandmother intended. And maybe that seems unfair to say, but it's clear that my grandmother intended to fight my father to the end. She'd fight them both, my father and her own daughter, to the death before she'd let my mother leave.

"My grandmother was was not going to have anything or anyone taken from her. That's what mattered. I'm sure. I don't know why. Maybe because she had already given up so much family, maybe because she had lost her brother, and husband, and whoever else she lost in those years we never hear about. I don't know. But I know that was the choice she gave my mother. I watched that. And even I knew that my grandmother would have fought till my mother was dead, Renie. I don't doubt it for a moment.

"My father was talking of moving once and I remember my grandmother coming to our house and asking my mother what she would do if she moved and had trouble and no family near. My mother told her she'd have my father. And my grandmother laughed. My grandmother never laughed, Renie, but she laughed at that. 'Your husband? You think you can depend on a husband? Who do you think is going to be giving you this trouble I'm talking about? What do you think I'm talking about, Mary?' My mother said she didn't know what my grandmother was talking about but my father was not going to be trouble, he never had been. He loved her. I remember my mother telling that to my grandmother, that my father loved her. And my grandmother laughed at that too and became angry. 'Listen,' she told my mother. 'I didn't raise any stupid children. And I raised you long enough with Hugh Logan, a man who drank away any money he ever had and who took whatever money he wanted from the rest of us to be gone as long as he wanted, I raised you long enough by myself for you to know what can happen, *what will happen!* And you think you can do that—raise three children by yourself with no family, *without me!* You've done nothing without me, your whole life, and you're not ready to start now. Believe me!'

"My mother was cornered but she fought. I watched her. I knew how afraid she was but I watched her fight, and I was proud of that—how my mother, even for a second, answered my grandmother, telling her, 'I'm as ready as you were when you left.' My mother knew she shouldn't have said that, she knew my grandmother was already near the edge of her tolerance for my mother's talk but she had been cornered and she'd fought back.

"My grandmother didn't yell. She seldom yelled. She stood there straight-backed and regal, looked my mother right in the face and told her something to break her; no matter how badly or irreparably it would break my mother, my grandmother used her most brutal blow. *'You'll never know what I left. Or what I've paid for leaving,'* she told my mother, *'But you'll know what can happen because I'll tell you.'* And then she did tell my mother something. I'm not sure what. It was the beginning of the end for my mother. It undid her. I saw that. My father saw that. He wasn't there to hear whatever my grandmother said, but he knew something had been done to my mother. He stopped fighting. But it was too late. My mother stopped painting, not right away, but eventually, and it had to do with what my grandmother was cruel enough to tell her.

"The day my mother stopped painting, she took her paintings, and some photographs and burned them. I saved what I could, I stole and hid what I could of the photographs. It was all crazy. That's what my mother finally felt I think. My father saw that too, and he backed away. He had no choice; it was his only way of not losing my mother completely, though he nearly did anyway because the struggle had gone on too long. But he let my mother know she didn't have to choose. He let her know that he'd stay even if my mother's loyalty or whatever she was handing over (it wasn't love) went to my grandmother. My mother pledged something (not love) to my grandmother, and my grandmother took it, knowing what it was and was not. It had to do with not abandoning something between them.

My mother's staying didn't have to do with not abandoning each other, because in many ways she and her mother had already done that. I think my mother's staying had to do with not abandoning parts of herself and whatever good there was in all my grandmother had indeed sacrificed of her own life for her daughters. Whatever good there had been my mother could not throw away, even for my father, or herself. She should have done it for herself, Renie. And I think now she has. But she couldn't then. My father saw that. And I think he saw too that for all my mother was handing over to my grandmother, my mother was promising my father even more. She promised him love because she really did feel that for him. But, with all these other pledges (none to herself), the pledge of love to my father wasn't enough to stop any of the pain. How can people ever think love's enough to stop the enormous possibilities for pain in this world?"

"What else is there?"

"I don't know. Nothing, I guess. Maybe that's what my mother found out. When she started painting those pictures of houses, she'd start with something small—a chair, and then she'd say, 'What room is this in, Norie?' while she began to paint a table, a kitchen table and then a woman at the table and then the light in the room and then sometimes she'd change the woman, how she looked, where she was, and my mother would ask, 'Who is she, Norie?' because she didn't seem to know, and she'd change the face, the eyes, the look in the eyes till it seemed right, till she recognized them. She'd blur the lines, and she'd tell me, *In life the lines are always blurred,* and the woman and the chair and the light and the look in the eyes were part of each other. And this felt right to my mother. For a while.

"Till she'd change things again. She'd take the same painting and she'd define the lines, the boundaries, the borders. She'd separate the pieces: the face and the chair and the light and the eyes, and then she'd try to put them back together again, into one picture but they didn't fit.

She'd cry: *Nothing fits. All the pieces and nothing fits!* She said she couldn't get it right. I didn't know what she wanted to get right. She'd change and change the picture, sometimes taking everything out of the painting but the woman, saying that everything else was blank, or sometimes she'd paint only the shell of a woman, with no features, and she'd say that even the woman was blank. She'd tell me that's the way things really were: *Empty, hollow outlines of things. It's all lies. And you better see that. For your own good.* She'd be very angry by then and not paint for a while. All she'd say then was, *I want to go home, Norie. I don't understand why we can't go home.* Maybe that was when she told me about living in the hospital dorms. My mother was about ten when she lost everything: her father, their house, even her mother, for a while. My grandmother left my mother and her sister with the nurses for a while.

"I guess my mother started to remember all this one day after she'd been painting around it for about a year, and maybe she knew she couldn't bear to remember anymore of it, and then there had already been that scene with my grandmother when my grandmother said whatever awful brutal thing she knew to say to break my mother, and my mother dragged all the paintings to the backyard. She was yelling for me to help her. I didn't want to, but she told me to take the pictures outside and when we had them all there, she got gasoline from the garage, threw a few matches on the pile, and watched them burn. She never painted again. That was about four years before the doctor came. Four years before my grandmother or father could tell what was happening—not before they knew, years before they could *tell* anyone, even the doctor."

Her head aches. "I've done very bad things."

"You were a little girl."

"I did them."

"What? What's so awful?"

Nora feels the words and the pictures inside her push to get out. They've been there for years, for all those years since she was ten and lost everything too—her mother, her childhood, herself. The pain behind her eyes is extraordinary. "My mother was in great pain and I did nothing. I stood and watched and did nothing. Nothing."

Nora sits up and pushes the blankets away as though clearing away the murky confusion from what she is saying. "One day, a few weeks before the doctor finally came for my mother, I walked into my mother's bedroom and I saw—" Nora feels the words cut. "I saw the small neat razor lying by my mother's hand. I just stood there. I didn't do anything, I didn't run to call my father at work, or my grandmother. I just stood there, thinking, *My mother's going to die.*"

And then before Nora knows what's happening, for one intricately cut second it seems possible for Nora to admit what she has never forgiven herself: "I left my mother lying in her own blood and went back to the living room and sat by the window, not because I thought she would want me to sit there, not because I thought I was being good or obedient or doing what I should—I knew what I was doing."

"You were in a nightmare. You were ten years old."

"Old enough." Nora says. Her grandfather told her, a five year old Nora, *The daoine sidhe will watch out for you if you deserve it.* That's all she had to do: deserve it. And she did, didn't she?

Don't leave me, Norie. That's all her mother asked.

And that's all I did, Nora thought for years, as if it were true.

V. The Daoine Sidhe Within

𝔑𝔬𝔯𝔞 is behind a door to which memory has brought an old (dead) enemy. Chained, the door is secure as it has been for years, though lately Nora has cracked it open for a second, hoping for memories she's wanted: of her grandfather, of times with her mother, with her father. Without warning, the enemy (who is also memory) pushes hard, as far as the chain will go. Nora slams herself against the door and is bruised. Her skin turns blue and purple where she is marked, where she will stay marked. She abandons the door, running in the other direction without looking back, without stopping. The enemy runs too, calling after her, almost in a whisper as if sending the breath down her throat. Threats ride on silence as much as sound. *Little girl,* the enemy calls as if Nora is still a little girl, as if she will run back to the door and swing it open, as if it will not close on her, like the lid on a coffin.

"My grandmother's anger is not an idle threat, Renie," Nora says, coming to the center of the thing, of everything. Renie sits near her on the sofa, trying to keep the blanket on Nora who moves it away. She is very warm, though at times chilled to the bone. At times Nora thinks it is the words which are chilling and burning her at the same time. "My grandfather used to accuse my grandmother of poisoning him. He checked himself into the hospital a few times and demanded they check for poison. Twice they found something suspicious but it wasn't anything they identified. She probably used rue or absinthe. If you use a lot of them, it's poison. She told me that once. We all knew that when my grandmother finally had had enough of my grandfather wandering off, she put a stop to it: she made him just sick enough to be going nowhere. You probably think I'm exaggerating but everyone knew about the tea.

"I'm sure my grandmother believed she did it for his own good, to keep him out of trouble, to keep the family together. She had many reasons, Renie. All selfless. I'm telling you my grandmother could make slipping rue in the tea seem a holy sacrament by the time she was done telling the story. Amazing really. I can just hear her: *'Oh, something had to be done. Anyone could see that. And who do you think was going to do it? Who in this house has the courage to see what's right and do it?'* And you'd see that she meant it, that she *could* do it, and then you'd remember that she'd made the tea you were drinking, and she'd see that thought cross your face and she'd tell you, *'Don't be worrying about yourself. That's only fennel you taste. I dropped a little in for the flavor is all. Such a lovely flavor. And fennel's very good for you, you know. Drink up.'* My grandmother's mother's cousin was quite an herbalist and healer herself, in Ireland, and I think my grandmother was about ten or so when she lived with this woman for a while, so my grandmother knows herbs. And my grandfather knows my grandmother. He always had the doctors check for poison. The thing is, what do doctors know about plants?

"It's all a puzzle." Nora says, feeling the pieces begin to fit. "Eugene's a big part of the puzzle, Renie. He's *in* the puzzle now because he's not outside, alive, trying to put it together. I think when he was trying to put things together, and nothing would fit, especially himself, he became angry and wanted to smash everything. He just wanted to put the whole damn puzzle over his head and throw it to the ground. He's still angry, Renie. He's dead six years and he's still angry. You think anger just ends? You think anger or fury or rage ends because a person dies?" Nora asks, wondering what she's talking about.

But then suddenly the wondering is over because everything—time, place, thought, feeling, *everything* has fallen in on Nora so that there is nothing between her and all the anger, nothing between her and Eugene. What she is saying now is coming from Eugene and all the anger that would not die. "When Eugene was about twelve, he crashed a car he'd stolen and was thrown through the windshield. His skull was broken in two places and his eyes were lacerated with glass." Nora flinches as if hit herself. "He was in the hospital for months and at some point a doctor checked his eyes. And recognized the dyslexia. That's why he had a hard time reading, not because he was stupid or lazy, not because he was evil, not because he deserved—" Nora grips her knees to rest her pounding head against them. "He was only a baby, Renie. My grandmother used to tell us, *All you have is family.* Maybe she meant it as a promise or a comfort, but we took it as a warning." Nora's eyes burn as if poison is pouring out of them. "My grandmother was seventeen or eighteen years old when she came alone to a strange country with no one and nothing. All we know is that she met a man, they married, had two daughters. We know he died. There are several stories about how. Once my grandmother told me he was killed working on a truck that fell on him and crushed his chest. Another time she told me a boulder fell on him as he was driving along a mountain road. Later, she told Hallie that he died in a fire, in a hotel. My mother said he died suddenly of a fever overnight. Whatever happened, he was just gone one day. That's what wounded my mother, I think. She told me she loved him very much. And I don't think she ever believed anyone would love her again. Maybe that's what my grandmother felt too. They couldn't believe that anyone in the world would love them again and they were standing right next to each other."

Renie stands by the fire, peeling an orange.

"It's all stories," Nora says, wondering after all these years what that means.

Renie comes near and hands Nora some orange.

Nora bites into the astounding flavor, realizing again how removed she's been from all senses, even taste. She takes another slice. "I'm so hungry," she says, sounding as if she doesn't believe something.

Renie laughs. "In three days you've eaten one bowl of soup and a slice of bread." Renie leaves the rest of the orange in a plate by Nora and sits in her chair. Nora feels protected now by the certainty that Renie knows something here. "What's the story of your mother's paintings?" she asks.

"I told you."

"Tell me again about the day your grandmother was there. What happened that day?"

"My grandmother?"

"The day she broke your mother? Don't you think that has something to do with your mother's pictures?"

Nora fights something here, then fights her own resistance to this memory which Renie knew would be there. "My mother was on to something years ago with her paintings, Renie, because her pictures started to scare my grandmother. I don't know why. But my grandmother was afraid to look at some of them. She didn't say that, of course. But my grandmother used to get angry when she looked at them. She'd stand in our dining room, in the clutter of canvas and tin cans, and she'd scratch at a splotch of paint that had spilled on the good dining room table and get angry, and I always thought it was at what she saw as my mother's sloppiness, at her neglect of what really mattered. My grandmother always wanted us to be neat and clean with ourselves, with our lives. But that's not what my grandmother was angry about, was it? It was that my mother was telling things, in all those pictures. It wasn't the mess of paint on the table. 'The good table,' my grandmother would say, shaking her head. It wasn't the good table at all that worried her—it was the pictures: all those pictures of—my God, Renie, my mother was painting from photographs," Nora remembers. "She had some photographs from when she was a child. She had pictures of her father, Renie. Not Granhugh, but her father. And she was painting from them." Nora wants to throw off blankets and fever and run anywhere but where she knows she is about to go.

"Photographs—my grandmother saw them one day when she was looking over my mother's drawings. Nonny was furious. She wanted them. She wanted all those photographs and my mother wouldn't give them to her. It was a horrible argument. And it frightened my mother. My grandmother didn't mention the photographs again, as if they didn't exist, as if she hadn't seen them, but her determination that my mother stop painting was relentless after that. Every day she came to our house and told my mother to stop this foolishness. She told my mother that she was wasting her time, that my mother had a house to run and children to take care of, and she shouldn't be wasting her time playing with paints. She said people were starting to talk about her. That it was dangerous. That people would think she couldn't take care of her house and children. She said my mother would lose everything. And she was right, Renie. My grandmother didn't know how right she was. My grandmother worried more about those paintings than she did about my mother. Nonny would have burned the paintings herself if my mother hadn't. Why? because of some old photographs that no one ever looked at? Why did my grandmother care about them?" Nora demands, wanting to pull back, overwhelmed by the sudden presence of her grandmother. She can tell it is really her grandmother's voice that is about to let go at her.

You want to know? You think you know so much. You know nothing! You think you children were never protected? You were protected from everything. I came here with nothing, knowing no one. I got off that boat not knowing where I would go. I left a country and family I loved because I wanted things I couldn't have. Not things you buy or see or touch but things you are. That's why I left.

Her grandmother, eighty-five and elegant, her silver hair twisted and pinned behind her beautiful head, imperious as ever, is here, sitting near her, calmly telling her, "I thought I'd find something for myself. And I did. You know what it was? The same thing that frightened me: no one knew me. The first time I realized that Nora, I felt as if I could fly: no one knew anything about me. I could choose anything for myself, about myself. I never felt so free, so much my own maker. It was probably a sin. You know what I did? I changed my name. Because I could choose a name, any I wanted. And I did. And then it was my name. Because I said it was. I never gave that up, Norie. With all that's happened, I've always kept that: if I say something, it's true. Because no one knows different. I wanted a place and a life I could barely imagine, where anything could happen, things I could never imagine.

"And they did. And I'm very sorry about some of them, but not all of them. I took care of myself. From the day I'm here, I've relied on no one. You think that's easy? You think I had anyone to protect me? I had nothing and no one. It was 1929, Norie. You've never lived in such a time, when there was nothing but hungry people getting hungrier everywhere you went. And no one knowing what to do about it. But I got a job in a hotel. Not with my own Irish name but with an American name, Judy Perkins, and I changed my voice, lost my brogue, as much of it as I could, and I didn't talk much because I had a job in a time when no one wanted Irish, when they put signs in the windows telling you that. A job. You can't imagine it. How wonderful that was—to work for nearly nothing, knowing I was lucky. I lived in one room for two years, mopping floors and making beds six and a half days a week, cleaning the same floors and bathrooms every day. I was seventeen years old. And some days very proud of myself for having a job and a room in a country where no one was taking care of me but myself. Some days I was very proud of that, and some days I wasn't. Some days I wanted nothing but to go home. I just wanted to go home, Norie. But there was no way back. It was like getting on a space ship, Norie, coming here. You think I didn't want to go home? Well, you think about wanting nothing more in your life than to go home and not being able to. You don't think that's real? How can you know what happened? You've always had a house to live in, haven't you? I made sure of that. I did that—no one else. You think anyone else cared about having a house? You think your grandfather cared? We moved thirty times with your grandfather before you were born, before I put a stop to it. I did what I had to. You think any of you would have a thing without me? Just ask your mother what I've given up. Just see how I've held this family together. I learned what it was to have no one. I learned. I had my brother for a while but I lost him too. Did anyone ever tell you that? Don't throw away what you can't get back, Norie.

"I'll tell you what it was like to have no one, you want to know so much: What happened, hah!

"Well, I met the hotel cook. I was seventeen and he was thirty-five, and he knew everything, I thought. He was so nice. But I was shy with him, you know. I didn't know how to talk to him when he asked how I was or if I liked the fancy chicken with all those sauces he cooked. I was so hungry I liked anything. He saw that: how hungry I was. And so, sometimes he'd give me a little extra food, telling me not to tell Mrs. Olin, the woman who had hired me, because we could both be fired, but he said I looked as though I needed the food and he gave it to me and we laughed with each other. We girls got two meals a day from the hotel—which was why it was such a good job, which was why we stayed, though we had to put up with a lot of not so good things from the managers. But I was lucky—the cook liked me, with my young face and red hair and freckles and way of knowing nothing about the world or men. Men like that. Never trust them, Nora. I tried to teach you girls that, my daughters and granddaughters. That was so bad? That's my great sin—teaching you not to trust? Well, that's the lesson I learned. And not from my grandmother. So, I'm sorry I tried to teach it to you before some man did. Because I really trusted and liked that cook who gave me extra food because I was so small and working so hard with no one to look after me. He liked that about me too.

And he kept liking me, and feeding me, and watching me and talking to me, and holding my hand, and touching my face, and turning my face around to him when I turned away because I'd never had anyone try to do what he was trying to do, and then doing (because I was hungry and if he could give me more food, he told me, he could also give me none). I looked at the plate of food as he did what he wanted. Whatever he wanted. As he did it all so easily because he could. So easily. And he said that if I complained he could and would say things about me to Mrs. Olin and she would fire me. Where would I go? I hope you are never that hungry.

Nora is stunned. Her grandmother has punched the fury out of her, without raising her voice.

And she isn't done.

So, you want to know more about your (real) grandfather? Didn't you think that was your grandfather? Did you think your grandfather was the man I married a year after that first baby, your mother, was born? No, that man, the first man I married, was Peg's father, but not your mother's. I always told them they had the same father, the only father they knew, the father they loved and who I loved, God help me, and who died, just died one day, without warning. Just gone. After ten years. Not long enough, but maybe more than I deserved. Just gone. Maybe I should have forgiven him a long time ago for that but I haven't. I can't even mention his name, I loved him so much, for loving me, Mary and all, that whole horrible time and all. And that's how he loved me, though he didn't know the things

I've just told you. Maybe I should have told you girls all about it long ago. God knows I haven't forgotten. God knows I see the whole thing every time I look at your mother. How do you think I felt at eighteen with her, that sin, swelling in me? When did you want me to sit you down with that story? When you were five or ten or fifteen?

Nora doesn't answer.

And when Nora does begin to answer, in this strange meeting between some part of herself and some part of her grandmother, she isn't sure what she is going to say, and she is surprised to hear herself tell her grandmother, *You were hungry. Hunger is not a sin! You didn't sin that night in the kitchen when you wanted to eat. When that man sinned against you. You have not loved us for that?*

Nora feels as though she is on a speeding train with her grandmother, shouting above the roaring engine, "It kept happening. Don't you see that? All the secrets kept my mother ashamed of things she didn't even know about herself. Till you told her. My God, you told her, didn't you? Just before Hallie was born, when my mother was painting from the photographs you didn't know she had. All my mother knew was that they were old photographs of people she didn't know, of people you knew, people you worked with when you first came here. Mostly they were pictures of women, all those women who scrubbed and cleaned every day together, who depended on each other to get through each day. That's who you said they were when she asked, when you saw the paintings and then saw the photographs pinned on a board so my mother could look at them while she painted. You tore them down and ripped a few, while my mother tore others out of your hands, and screamed at you to leave her work alone. I had never heard my mother scream at you before. It scared both us us. You were probably scared too, but mostly you seemed angry. You told my mother she didn't know what she was doing, painting those awful things.

"'What things? What are you talking about? It's just pictures of some people,' my mother said, still believing you would never hurt her the way you were about to. You told her what things you were talking about, didn't you? That's how I remember this. I heard you tell her: 'That monster there,' you said, pointing to some hazy image of a man among a group of people around a big cooking table in a hotel kitchen, 'that monster there is your father.'

"My mother looked. I stayed where I was at the other end of the table. But my mother looked at the photograph and seemed puzzled. 'That's not my father,' she said. 'It doesn't even look like him.'

"'How would you know? You never met him.' And then you told her why. Without a tear or bit of feeling for either one of you right then, you told my mother the story you just told me. That's when I first heard this. When you told my mother, 'Believe me, your father was a monster.' You were calm by then, in control again as my mother unraveled, as you unraveled the story for her, around her. Maybe the first entirely true story you'd told in years, and you used it to hurt her; you'd saved it to hurt her. I hated you at that moment, not understanding what you were talking about, but knowing my mother wouldn't recover from it. And that you didn't care. I wanted to tell you to stop. I wanted to make you stop. But I did nothing. I watched you hurt and hurt her, my mother, and I did nothing. That's what I always do, what I can never forgive myself for doing. Nothing, for my mother, or Eugene, or myself. Over and over. It has to end!"

Nonny is affected by none of this. *I did what I had to,* she told Nora. *And I'll do it again. You don't know everything.*

"I know I'm afraid of you."

Well, that's not the worst thing in the world to be afraid of, little girl.

"You're burning up," Renie says, her hand going to Nora's forehead, feeling cool to Nora who closes her eyes, her head and throat hurting as if the heat behind her eyes will explode except that it is sliding down and scorching her throat. Renie hands her two aspirins and a glass of the coldest water Nora has ever swallowed. "It's all the poison pouring out of me," Nora says.

"Well, it's been in there a long time." Renie is sitting by the fire.

"My grandmother had courage, Renie," Nora says, finding the part of the story she knows is true. *"That's* what got my grandmother on that ship, with no one beside her. She just got on that ship, for all the possibilities that were probably already gone. That's what she's never forgiven any of us. As though we took them from her."

Nora understands the rage.

Nora wakes up, reaching for Renie: "I broke the glass vase, Renie. It fell off the kitchen counter when I reached for something. I shouldn't have done that. We were supposed to behave ourselves till Nonny got home. I was by myself and I thought no one would know if I ate something. I was hungry. The same as my grandmother. I was hungry. I thought no one would know if I just got something from the counter. I didn't turn on the light. The glass vase fell off the counter into a thousand pieces on the floor. In my grandmother's kitchen. And then I heard footsteps upstairs. I didn't know anyone was home. I didn't smell Granhugh's tobacco. Then I knew it wasn't Granhugh. I knew even before he came into the kitchen and caught me trying to clean up the glass. It began with the glass, because I broke the glass, and he heard that—" Nora flinches, immediately putting her hand to her mouth, her sound shaking, cracking, then almost of itself this begins again, "The glass broke, I was on the floor trying to pick it up and he was just there, Renie. Eugene's father, Gil Delaney."

In a sudden movement that seems to come from somewhere outside herself, Nora gets up from the sofa, reaches across the coffee table and slides the glass vase to the floor. Glass is everywhere— glass and water and flowers everywhere. Nora is on the floor trying to pick everything up. She has to clean it all up so none of this will happen again. If she cleans it up now none of this will happen again.

She feels someone touch her wrist. Renie. Renie is on the floor too, reaching over Nora's lap for the glass—is that what hurts? what's slicing into the blood that's crawling down Nora's arm?

"Let it go," Renie says softly. She is sitting with Nora on the floor, telling Nora to let go of the glass. But Nora knows she has to shut her hand tighter around the pain or everything will fall apart again.

"Drop the glass, Nora."

"I can't."

"Drop the glass, Nora. Here—" Renie says, trying to open her hand.

"No."

"Give me the glass."

There is blood on Nora's nightgown. She wants to open her hand but she can't. "I can't—God, Renie, *please,* I can't—"

"Let it go," Renie shouts and Nora thinks it's the shouting, the screaming inside herself that Renie is saying to let go, to let go of the glass voice, the sound Nora has been trying for more than twenty years to keep very quiet inside herself so it will not shatter everything. That's what Nora wanted to do when she saw her uncle standing there, drunk, in her grandmother's kitchen, thinking she was his wife Peg. He was calling her Peg and trying to hit her and all Nora had to do was say something. Why didn't she say something? Why couldn't she make a sound? Renie is saying to let it go? to scream? Now? The same scream now? It is the same scream, still there, as ineluctable as it was twenty years ago and as frightening—a scream so terrible it would shatter all the voices.

"Let it go, Nora," Renie orders because she does not care now if Nora is scared. Renie is scared too because Nora is clutching the glass, crushing it into herself—not screaming.

Pushing against her, Renie opens Nora's hand. Nora watches. The little piece of glass has dug deeply into the palm of her hand. "I didn't mean to break it. I didn't." Nora screams past the burning as Renie kneels over her, putting her arms around her, surrounding her, but Nora pulls away. "I watched my mother that day when she was cut and bleeding. I watched her as calmly as my grandmother watched Eugene die, and I went back to the living room and I waited. What right did I have to save myself when I wouldn't save my mother? I couldn't make a sound when he pushed me, then hit me—I was bruised, that's what my grandmother saw, the bruise. And a few days later she told us Kath and Sheila's father was dead. And I was glad."

"You didn't kill him—"

Nora laughs. "I know that. No one killed him. He's not dead. I saw him the other day. He came to my apartment. I answered the door and he was there, Renie. I thought he was dead. But he was standing there. *Hi, Nora, think I was dead?* I kept staring at him through the glass. I couldn't move. I didn't say anything. I kept staring at him. *I just want to talk to you. Just let me in so I can talk to you*, he was saying. How could he be there, Renie? He wanted to come in and see me. I thought he was dead and he wanted to come in. Then I knew he was alive and I had to hold the door closed. I bolted the door and got dressed. Then I ran. I ran out the back."

Nora feels as if she's in a tunnel with all these voices, these sharp pieces of glass sounds circling her. Her arms are folded around herself, tightly, as she sits on the floor in the water and the glass, moving back and forth, in the tunnel, telling Renie what she can, "My grandmother knew he was alive because she sent him away. He was too dangerous—first my Aunt Peg and then his own children and then me. He was killing all of us. So she killed him. She told us he was dead. That was her story. We were all in it the minute she told us. Maybe we believed it; maybe we didn't. *Where was the funeral? How did he die?* No one asked. No one cared. We were in the story we wanted to be in: Gil was gone forever, dead. That's what we wanted. We all got what we wanted, real or not. But we *were* in the real world too and even though she had killed him for us and made us think we were safe, we never were. *Never!* How safe was Eugene? What the hell happened to Eugene? That's what I thought the minute I saw Gil standing there: *My God, he killed Eugene and now he's come back for me.* That's why I ran."

Nora is sitting on the floor, glass and blood on her hands. She knows that even though Renie has taken the glass from her hand, if she presses a little harder she will feel that high sharp pain and she is tempted to press. To get it over with. She wants all the pain over with. "You know, Renie, for years I thought I was crazy because a few times after we were told that Gil was dead I saw him. He must have come back—one time I saw him fighting with Eugene in the snow in my grandmother's backyard. It was very early in the morning. I was by myself. I heard noises and I looked out the back window and there was Eugene—he was about fourteen, fighting with someone I recognized, his father, knocking his father (who was dead) into a mound of snow. I saw the blood in the snow later. I never said anything to anyone. That might make it true and I wanted him dead. And a few years later, I saw Eugene fight the same man. I'd gone over to my grandmother's before school, very early, I don't even remember why now. I remember going up my grandmother's driveway and seeing Eugene and my uncle fighting. I recognized Gil. I knew who he was, and he saw me too. He looked right at me, and I ran. I didn't help Eugene. I didn't care about Eugene. He could take care of himself. That's what I told myself. And I was glad he was beating up his father. I went back down the driveway, glad that Eugene was pounding him. But three days later Eugene was dead."

"You didn't kill Eugene."

Nora can't believe that, because as sure as she is that there is blood on her now, she knows she saw that blood in the show and should have told . . . someone . . . and so she tells Renie again, "Three days later—" looking at Renie who stays where she is, very near, waiting for Nora to feel safe enough to hold on. Nora isn't sure she ever will, but then not knowing how, she does. And Renie tells her again, "You did not kill Eugene," Nora hearing the words as answer to a prayer, ancient and her own.

"I haven't let all this happen," she says, nearly as a question, keeping her eyes on Renie, unsure what she believes, culpability too old and deep and gnarled to vanish in first confession. "Kathleen thinks there was something in the whiskey, in the bottle she saw in Eugene's room the morning he died. My grandmother could have done that— not to kill Eugene but she could have done that. She knew about soaking seeds to extract poison. Make *scailtin* strong enough, it'll kill you. She might have meant it for Gil, to make him sick, very sick. He was a big man. You measure differently for a boy, even a strong boy like Eugene. It was Gil she meant to stop. Who knew Eugene would drink it? Who knew any of this would happen?"

But the words double back, pulling and pulled by their own shadows. "We all knew. Somehow we all knew," Nora admits. She rubs her eyes and smears blood and water on her face. "Whatever happened to Eugene was an accident. A tragic, foolish accident. But it killed him." Nora is amazed at the strength of the voice coming out of her, and at something else, something strong and insisting and hers: sorrow, an unimaginable sorrow for them all.

And just when she might have thought this sound and sorrow were her discovery, an old wise voice circles and tells her again, *Transformation and healing, ancient cures.* She thinks of Granhugh's story, of the little boy dancing himself into the beautiful strong full black bird as shadows cross the room and Renie wipes the blood from her hands.

Other books from Livingston Press

Fiction

Tom Abrams, *A Bad Piece of Luck,* novel, ISBN 0-942979-23-0, $9.95

W.C. Bamberger, *A Jealousy for Aesop,* stories, ISBN 0-930501-13-6, $9.95

James E. Colquitt, editor, *Alabama Bound: Contemporary Stories,* ISBN 0-942979-26-5, $13.95

Natalie L.M. Petesch, *Wild with All Regret,* stories, ISBN 0-930501-07-1, $10.95

Louis Phillips, *Hot Corner: Baseball Stories and Humor,* ISBN 0-942979-36-2, $11.95

B. K. Smith, *Sideshows,* stories, ISBN 0-942979-16-8, $12.95

William F. Van Wert, *Don Quickshot,* novel in verse, ISBN 0-942979-32-X, $9.95

Allen Woodman, *Saved by Mr. F. Scott Fitzgerald,* stories, ISBN 0-942979-41-9, $9.95

Allen Woodman, *The Shoebox of Desire,* stories, ISBN 0-930501-11-X, $ 8.95 *(Note: all these stories are included in the previous book—artwork by Ross Zirkle is not.)*

Poetry

Cory Brown, *A Warm Trend,* ISBN 0-930501-19-5, $8.95

Michael J. Bugeja, *Flight from Valhalla,* ISBN 0-942979-12-5, $9.95

Cynthia Chinelly, *Coralroot,* ISBN 0-942979-01-X, $5.00 (chapbook)

Stephen Corey, *The Last Magician,* ISBN 0-930501-17-9, $9.95

Stephen Corey, *Synchronized Swimming,* ISBN 0-942979-14-1, $9.95

B.H. Fairchild, *The Arrival of the Future,* ISBN 0-930501-01-8, $8.95

Charles Ghigna, *Speaking in Tongues,* ISBN 0-942979-20-6, $11.95

Ralph Hammond, editor, *Alabama Poets,* ISBN 0-942979-07-9, $12.95

R.T. Smith. *The Cardinal Heart,* ISBN 0-942979-09-5, $8.95

R.T. Smith, *Hunter-Gatherer,* ISBN 0-942979-34-6, $9.95

Eugene Walter, *Lizard Fever,* ISBN 0-942979-18-4, $12.95
        (illustrated by author)

Michael Waters, *The Barn in the Air,* ISBN 0-942979-00-1, $5.00

Just Published!

L.A. Heberlein

SiXteen **R**easons Why i

Killed **R**ichar**D** M. Ni**X**on

a novel.

It was in the spring and early summer of 1974, when the impeachment was gearing up, that I started getting the Nixon calls. People would call in and confess to having killed Nixon. . . . So begins the calm narration of this novel, but underneath, the story jangles—just as did the Nixon era—and we are treated to wild confessions of shooting down the President's plane with a shoulder-launched missile, of nicotine-starved aliens inadvertently causing Nixon's death, of a prescient doctor who ended matters on the birthing table . . . and a Nixon Koan for Zen fans.

ISBN 0-942979-30-3, paper, $ 9.95

Recently Released!

Tom Abrams

A Bad Piece of Luck

a novel.

"*. . . will appeal to people who are comfortable with Tom Robbins and William Faulkner with a healthy dash of Erskine Caldwell. . . .*"

—St. Petersburg Times

"*Abrams' use of image to convey the story is present in every page.*"

—Tampa Tribune

"The name of the place was The Cadillac Bar. It was the kind of a bar you'd go to early and forget to eat. You was kind of tough, or a little crazy, or you was in the process of hardening up. Or maybe some friends said they'd meet you here, but they ain't showed yet, and you're sitting at a table feeling out of place.

The people around you are thieves and whores, cowboys, bikers, off-duty cops—they're on parole, underage, they're all tricked out in their finest. Or say, look at the old lady with the bowling shirt on, her face expressing the sorrow of three widows. . . ."

from *A Bad Piece of Luck*

ISBN 0-942979-23-0, paper, $9.95

Reviewed in *the New York Times* . . .

Allen Woodman

Saved
by Mr. F. Scott Fitzgerald
and other stories

"In this charming collection of stories, Allen Woodman . . .
captures the special qualities of particular moments, finding the important in the trivial. He reminds us that life is not
made up of great events, that daily routines and chance
encounters provide the real fiber of human existence"
   Christopher Atamian, in *The New York Times*

ISBN 0-942979-41-9
$9.95 paper

Forthcoming from Livingston Press:

Peter Huggins

Hard Facts

"In His deft, witty, learned poems, Peter Huggins treats hard facts with a delightful, deceptive ease. He is able to do so because he is, after all, that rarity among poets, a good writer of graceful sentences. Such clear language handled with such a light touch welcomes the reader into the world of the poem; after all, Huggins wants us to see and to understand as brightly and truly as he does. In poem after poem we do."

—Thomas Rabbit

"This first collection of poems by Peter Huggins reveals a distinctive new Southern voice. His poems pass freely from registers of homegrown surrealistic wit to intensities of feeling, plainly expressed: he is capable of making high comedy out of the dead who return to vote in our elections and of mourning the living, who "take/ Their place among a thousand weary stars." This is a book to read and read again."

—Charles Martin

Available in Spring of 1998

ISBN 0-942979-44-3, paper, $9.95
ISBN 0-942979-43-5, cloth, $19.95

Photo: Patricia Kennedy

Maureen McCafferty lives in Queens, New York, and travels, whenever she can, in Ireland where her father was born and most of the McCaffertys, including 54 first cousins, live. She has a Doctor of Arts in Creative Writing from Syracuse University. Her fiction and poetry have appeared in many literary journals, including *American Writing, Rhino, Clockwatch Review,* and the anthology *A Patchwork of Dreams: Voices from the Heart of New America. Let Go the Glass Voice* is her first novel.